"C
the r
had l ..., languidly toward
the hearth.

He licked at dry lips. His heart pounded. This wasn't what he'd expected.

Jamie smiled at him. "Look at the fire with me . . . how it's dancing with joy. Don't be afraid. . . ."

"Oh, I'm not afraid." His voice was a husky growl. "But perhaps I'd better stay over here."

"I have something to tell you."

His blood was racing, his breath coming quick and harsh. But it was like hearing the sirens' song. He was suddenly powerless, his resistance weakened.

"Come here," she whispered once more, knowing she wouldn't have to say it again.

When he moved within inches of her, when he bent his head and kissed her mouth, when he took her in his arms, Jamie understood what she hadn't until this moment. This was her destiny. . . .

WHAT ARE *LOVESWEPT* ROMANCES?

They are stories of true romance and touching emotion. We believe those two very important ingredients are constants in our highly sensual and very believable stories in the LOVESWEPT *line. Our goal is to give you, the reader, stories of consistently high quality that may sometimes make you laugh, sometimes make you cry, but are always fresh and creative and contain many delightful surprises within their pages.*

Most romance fans read an enormous number of books. Those they truly love, they keep. Others may be traded with friends and soon forgotten. We hope that each LOVESWEPT *romance will be a treasure—a "keeper." We will always try to publish*

LOVE STORIES YOU'LL NEVER FORGET BY AUTHORS YOU'LL ALWAYS REMEMBER

The Editors

Loveswept® 724

SPELLBOUND

ADRIENNE
STAFF

BANTAM BOOKS
NEW YORK · TORONTO · LONDON · SYDNEY · AUCKLAND

SPELLBOUND
A Bantam Book / January 1995

LOVESWEPT and the wave design are registered trademarks of Bantam Books, a division of Bantam Doubleday Dell Publishing Group, Inc. Registered in U.S. Patent and Trademark Office and elsewhere.

ISBN 0-553-44350-X

Published simultaneously in the United States and Canada

Bantam Books are published by Bantam Books, a division of Bantam Doubleday Dell Publishing Group, Inc. Its trademark, consisting of the words "Bantam Books" and the portrayal of a rooster, is Registered in U.S. Patent and Trademark Office and in other countries. Marca Registrada. Bantam Books, 1540 Broadway, New York, New York 10036.

PRINTED IN THE UNITED STATES OF AMERICA

OPM 0 9 8 7 6 5 4 3 2 1

ONE

Slowly the clouds moved across the bright face of the full moon. Mysterious shadows cloaked the building where Jamie Payton tried to paint. For an instant it was as though the stage was purposely being dimmed; the scene was being set. Jamie felt a chill walk across her skin. She had the strangest feeling that something was about to happen, something unexplainable, something unforeseen. Something . . .

The lights went out. One minute Jamie was staring at her half-finished painting, brush in hand, and the next . . . total darkness.

"Damn!" She felt her way over to the wall near the door and flicked the light switch once, twice. Nothing. What was going on? Moving cautiously, she walked around the wall to the windows, covered with heavy oilcloth to keep out the distractions of the city while she painted. She slid a fingernail under the rim of a thumbtack, the cloth sprang up, and light poured in.

The street lamps were on outside and there were lights in the row of storefronts across the way. Jamie frowned. She opened the window, leaned out, and saw that lights were shining from the windows in her own building as well. Damn! Wouldn't you know? Just when she thought she was finally getting somewhere with her painting, something bad had to happen. It was probably the wiring in her loft or a blown fuse. But why now? Why her?

Tugging her fingers through her uncombed hair, she turned back to the darkness of her own room. For a moment she stood there immobilized by a childhood sense of dread, feeling the old ghosts closing in. But she shook them off and moved quickly through the loft, pulling open one drawer after another in search of candles. Her elbow hit the corner of a box, the vase on top teetered, and an entire still life crashed to the floor.

Jamie screamed. She didn't mean to; it just happened before she could control herself.

Biting her lip, she bent and began picking glass shards off the worn wood floor. She was just reaching for another when there was a knock at the door.

"Now what?" she groaned. She was tempted to ignore it, but whoever was out there was very persistent. Setting the broken glass down in a neat pile, she walked over, checked the chain lock, and opened the door a few inches.

"Yes?" she said, peering out into the corridor. The guy standing there looked familiar, a neighbor most likely.

"Hi. I'm Kent. From next door," he added, confirming her guess. "I didn't mean to bother you, but I heard a crash, and a scream. . . ." He shrugged. "I just wanted to check that everything's okay."

Jamie gave him a thin smile. "I'm fine. Thanks. That was nice of you, but I'm okay."

He stood there.

"Really," she insisted. "My lights went out and I bumped into some things I'd left lying around. I'm a painter and—"

"I know," he interrupted. "Abstracts. You told me a year ago when we first met. And I'm the actor from next door, the one who used to play his music too loud."

"Oh yes, of course I remember," she lied, feeling really embarrassed now. He *was* trying to be neighborly. "Well, perhaps sometime you could come over and we could talk about our work."

He smiled. "You said that also. But you didn't show up at my New Year's Eve party. Or my St. Patrick's Day bash . . . green beer and all. I was hurt."

Jamie stiffened. "I must have been busy. I'm sorry."

"It's okay." He smiled. "I just thought we could be friends."

"Yes. That's nice. And thanks again for being the good Samaritan."

"No problem. Hey—just call if you need any help."

"Yes, I will. Thanks. Good night."

She shut the door and leaned back against it, feeling oddly shaken. The truth was, she could have used a little help right now. But it was just as true that she couldn't ask. Ever. Before she could stop herself, she was always saying, "No, thank you, I'm fine; I don't need anything." It was just the way she was.

Pain squeezed her heart. She wanted to be different. She longed to be different, to be open, warm, and responsive, to be the kind of person who was surrounded by friends. It would be wonderful to be the center of smiles and laughter, the giver and recipient of hugs.

Jamie's throat tightened around forbidden tears. She pushed away from the door, away from her thoughts. "Now where the hell did I put those candles?"

Finally she had two lit and placed strategically in the dimness. Tomorrow she'd complain to her landlord. She'd have it out with him once and for all. He could either fix things so that she could paint without interruption or he could find himself another tenant. She'd move. She'd find another loft in Georgetown, or somewhere else in D.C. The classifieds probably had dozens of listings.

Reaching for an old newspaper, she knocked a week's worth of mail onto the floor. When everything finally fluttered to a stop, there on top was a bill from the electric company, FINAL NOTICE typed across the envelope in bold print.

The electric company! Her hand flew to her mouth. The telephone company! Her rent! She'd forgotten to pay all her bills. She'd been so determined to finish this latest painting that she'd forgotten everything else. And for what? She still couldn't get it right. She couldn't achieve the power she wanted, the dynamic tension of form and shadow. She couldn't capture the light, that perfect but elusive light she saw in her imagination. But she was damned if she was going to give up. Hurrying to the easel, she picked up her brush, dipped it in paint. . . .

At that instant a gust of wind blew in through the open windows and snuffed out her candles.

It was too much; she couldn't stand it anymore. Problems were piling on top of problems: the poor sales at her first one-woman show, then this painting, and now the lights—

She was going to cry. She knew it, hating herself for it, fighting against it. And even as the tears gathered she heard her father's cold voice with its chill disapproval, its utter disdain: "Look at you. Out of control. Are you crying? Are those tears? What are you, a baby? A failure? A loser?"

His ghost chased her from the loft.

Jamie took the stairs two at a time, grabbing at the banister for balance. She ran out the front door and into the loud, impersonal noise of the street with its car radios, college students, and flood of tourists. Above her head, the sky was filled with strange, leaden clouds that seemed to catch the noise and bounce it back down like an echo chamber. But even this was better than that voice.

Jamie stuffed her hands into the pockets of her jeans and walked on, head down. It started to drizzle. Every store light, every car light, every traffic light flashing green/yellow/red was reflected on the wet canvas of the side-walks. The lights streaked and spread. They flowed in elongated, mystical shapes. They arched into rainbows at the edges of curbs where oil and grease had been laid like wax crayon on gray paper. Colors and light, light and color— Why couldn't she paint like this, with such random beauty, such freedom?

Drawing a shaky breath, Jamie tilted her face up to the rain. It made it easier to hide the tears.

She wandered along, turning right or left without thought. Night fell over the city and the stores closed. As the rain picked up, the streets emptied. But Jamie was reluctant to go home, home to the darkness, the silence, her own thoughts . . . and that awful voice.

Pulling up the hood of her sweatshirt, she took a sharp left down a narrow, dark street she'd never seen before. Suddenly everything looked unfamiliar. Yet she almost felt, in her confusion and despair, as if her feet had led her surely to this place. But why?

One light shone up ahead, spilling a welcoming pool of yellow warmth out onto the sidewalk. The sign on the window was old and faded, the paint worn away: MYST R UM. The window was full of the strangest things: antique toys, rhinestone earrings, a feather boa and a silk top hat, cut-glass vases, a shawl with red silk thread and ten-inch fringes. They were odd, mismatched items but beautiful to an artist's eye. Already Jamie was picturing how she could stand a vase on one end of the shawl, its fringe hanging down off the table's edge as sunlight splintered through the glass. She could use layer upon layer of paint to create a jeweled, almost enameled effect.

Abandoning herself to her imagination, Jamie entered the store's dim interior. Chaos reigned. Things were stacked everywhere in a topsy-turvy jumble. This store is as out of control as my loft, she thought, and almost smiled. She drew her fingers along the dusty countertops, traced the facets on a tiny vase, peered into the ancient, beveled-glass cases, gathered into her hands dry, threadbare fabrics that rustled under her touch.

"Welcome."

Jamie spun in surprise. She searched the recesses of the store for the source of the man's voice, but jumped nonetheless as he stepped out of the shadows. He was a tiny old man with a mane of white hair and a knowing smile. "Good evening. I'm so glad you've come."

She nodded. "I bet you don't have many customers on a night like tonight."

"It only takes one. The right one," the man replied, a glint in his eye.

Taken aback, Jamie quickly shook her head. "Oh, I'm afraid you're going to be disappointed. I don't want anything."

"Don't you?" He held her eyes. "Oh, I think neither of us is going to be disappointed this evening. Come over here. Look what I have for you."

She hesitated, frowning. Living in Georgetown, she was used to meeting the occasional odd character, but she had the strangest feeling about this man—

Squaring her shoulders, she strode across the store. "What is it you'd like to show me? I really don't need any jewelry, and I don't collect antiques."

"Nevertheless, these are for you." Reaching down into the dusty case, the man drew out an old, handpainted box. The hinge squeaked as he lifted the lid. Inside were two neat, perfect rows of paints, twelve tubes all tightly capped, all waiting to be used.

Without thinking, Jamie ran a fingertip along the top row, slowly, sensually, in wonder and delight. The tubes felt warm, alive, as if transmitting some strange energy. Biting her lip, she was already imagining how it would feel to squeeze the paint onto her palette, dip in the curved sable of her brush, draw that first magical stroke across a white and empty canvas.

Suddenly she yanked her hand back. "What makes you think I'd be interested in these?"

"Aren't you?" The old man gave a Cheshire-cat smile.

"I don't know. Maybe, maybe not. But you didn't answer my question."

He shrugged, lowered his eyes, and busied himself with a tray of glass beads. "Perhaps I was wrong. Perhaps instead you'd like to browse—"

"No, I'll take the paints," she answered, shutting the box top with trembling fingers. "Yes, I'll take them. How much are they?"

"One dollar."

"What?" She laughed, caught by surprise.

"One dollar. A special for the woman who says there's nothing she wants . . . because she doesn't know what it is she needs."

"Now wait just a minute—"

"Take them," he interrupted imperiously, then bobbed his head up and down, becoming again just a smiling old man. "Take them. You'd be doing me a favor. Now they're fresh and bright, but they'll just sit here on the shelf and dry up, all their possibilities gone to waste. Certainly you can make better use of them than that."

"Yes," Jamie said softly, eager to hold them in her hands. "But can't I pay you a fair price? I feel like I'm cheating you."

"No, my dear, you are pleasing me. Think of them as being meant for you."

He was working as he spoke, wrapping the box in brown paper, tying it with twine. He handed it to her, and again she caught that glint of mischief and mystery in his eyes.

Jamie felt her cheeks flush. Holding the package to her chest, she handed him the dollar, then hurried to the door. "Thank you," she whispered with a quick glance back over her shoulder. "Thanks." Then she stepped out into the rain.

One stop at the store on the corner for more candles and she was back at the loft.

Fitting the key into the lock, she pushed the door open into darkness.

"Let there be light!" she quipped, striking a match.

Around her, piles and stacks and walls full of canvases took shadowy form. She set a candle on the windowsill, one on the kitchen table, one on her night table. Then she sat down and unwrapped the package.

The box itself was old, the wood worn to a smooth, polished veneer; the painting on the lid was faded and dim. But inside, the twelve perfect tubes of paint lay fresh and shining, each wrapped in shiny white paper, foreign words labeling them in a tiny, perfect hand. She couldn't read their message, but that didn't matter. One twist of their tops and the paint would spill out: ocher, burnt umber, cerise, cadmium yellow, saffron, Prussian blue, lamp black, white . . . each one more beautiful than anything real. As beautiful as dreams and wishes.

Her heart pounding with anticipation, Jamie put a fresh canvas on the easel. She would start now, right now. She wouldn't waste a moment, not a second. This time she'd get it right. She would.

As she opened the paints light and shadow flickered in her imagination; images she had never considered came together. Rather than planning a design, she could feel it emerging, gathering form and power, racing from her brain to her fingertips like some irrepressible impulse.

Brush in hand, she made one sure stroke. Another. Letting the paint take her, she seemed almost to dream the form, the images of the painting she'd make. It was like entering into a trance: letting go of reality and slipping into another state, another consciousness . . . moving deeper and deeper toward some mysterious destination. Her hand moved of its own will. Colors appeared. Shapes blurred and shifted. The paint flowed, caressing the rough texture of the canvas. The canvas warmed, coming to life beneath the kiss of brush and paint.

And then a yawn shook her, and another right behind it. Glancing at the clock, Jamie couldn't believe what time it was! She'd been painting for hours without stopping, almost without breathing. Suddenly she couldn't keep her eyes open. Her eyelids were heavy; even her eyelashes felt tired. She cleaned her brushes, blew out the candles, and fell into bed. And for the first time in longer than she could remember, her sleep was free of nightmares.

14

The next evening, far across town, Edward Rockford stood in his bedroom, staring at his reflection in the mirror. Something seemed to hold him there against his will. He knew it was crazy but he had the strangest feeling that a shadow, an image, had flickered there behind his own, *within* his own.

"Damn." The muttered curse escaped through clenched teeth. His jaw ached with tension. Scowling, he shook his head to clear his thoughts, but they remained as dark and brooding as they had been for months, for years. It seemed like forever.

And tonight? He did not want to be going out tonight. He didn't think he could endure another meaningless society event, another stifling room filled with chattering people. Just thinking of it made him tug at the knot of his tie, the top button of his starched shirt. His dark eyes flashed with anger and frustration. There would be no companionship there, nothing of any substance. It would merely be another evening spent among strangers, filled with hollow laughter and shallow talk. It was driving him crazy. Crazy! He could feel his passion, his true self, stretch and circle in its cage, pace the narrow limits, strain against its confines. He could feel its claws pierce his heart, his soul.

But no!

Staring straight ahead, holding his own dark gaze, he fought the passion down. Stilled it. Lashed it tight to the bars of his muscle and bone, the cage he had forged out of will and despair.

Why go? Why bother? I'll stay here. Pour a drink. Read. I won't go.

But something drove him on, restless, seeking. And tonight that feeling was stronger than ever, fierce and compelling. But to what? What hope? What dream?

Fool!

He smiled a cold, bitter smile, a mocking smile so chilling it would have raised goose bumps on the arms of the women waiting for him in the car downstairs. *If* they had seen. Which they never would.

"Never," he whispered, erasing all emotion from his face, all feeling from his dark, dark eyes.

And, looking as cool and soulless as a painting, he shrugged into his jacket and left.

At that same moment the phone rang in Jamie's silent loft. It made her jump. Brush still in hand, she walked over to where the phone lay on the floor next to the bed. "Hello?"

"Jamie? Hello, this is Kent. From next door?"

"Yes, hi. How are you?" She shifted from one foot to the other, impatient already.

"I'm great. And I'm about to make you an offer you can't refuse. My friend's got three tickets to the opening tonight at Lupercine. It's their photography show. Great stuff! So you're coming with us. Be ready in an hour."

Jamie shook her head. "I can't. Thank you but—"

"No ifs, ands, or buts. You'll love it, and you can't play the hermit forever. Say yes."

"No, I really can't. I'm in the middle of painting and I don't want to stop. But it was very nice of you to think of me. I appreciate it."

"Sure. You know what? I'll just slip the extra ticket under your door. Use it if you can. Bye."

"Good-bye."

Jamie stared at the receiver for a moment, then set it down, frowning. She had been painting all morning and afternoon, caught in the same trancelike state as the night before, and this interruption annoyed her. The last thing she needed was some enamored neighbor lurking at her door. As if she was anticipating his unwelcome appearance in that very spot, her gaze swept the room.

She gasped, her eyes flying wide.

Across the room, her canvas looked gorgeous, vibrant, alive with a shimmering light that seemed to come from within it, from the paint itself. She stood dumbfounded, transfixed. *That* was the light she'd imagined, the light she'd seen before only in her dreams. There . . . there in *her* painting!

Unaware of her own movement, she took one step closer. Maybe it was only a trick of light coming in through the windows, some crazy mix of smog and sun. Maybe she was dreaming it now. She rubbed her eyes, getting paint in her hair and on her forehead, but she didn't feel a thing. The light remained. A beautiful light, a perfect light . . .

But a *landscape*.

On the canvas, unforeseen and unplanned, a scene was taking shape: a sweep of hills, trees, a building of some kind hinted at by sharp, dark strokes of umber. It seemed barely hidden beneath her usual abstract style. The brush strokes were hers, as familiar as her own signature. The colors were hers, her characteristic overlay of thin layers of bright hues. But . . . a landscape?

She hadn't painted a landscape since her first formal art class when her father had walked into the studio, glanced over her shoulder, and passed judgment: "Well, you don't have much of an aptitude for that technique, do you?"

That had hurt. It still did. So she certainly had no intention of painting a landscape now . . . or ever.

But is it possible to paint something you don't even know you're painting? she wondered. Goose bumps rose on her arms.

She approached the easel warily. She drew a deep breath.

Biting nervously at her lower lip, she reached for the brush. But suddenly it felt cold and dead in her hand and her hand was shaking. It took all her energy just to screw the caps on the tubes of paint and to clean her brushes. And soon the loft would be dark.

Maybe she *should* go out for a little while. A bath first, a bite to eat, and then the opening. Suddenly it seemed like exactly the right thing to do. Hurrying into the bathroom, she ran the water good and hot, added some bath salts, and then sank through the cool bubbles into the heat and comfort with a sigh. Closing her eyes, she kept her mind carefully empty. No thoughts. No fears. No dreams. Nothing.

So she was completely unaware of what was about to begin . . . or had already begun.

TWO

Jamie could see the lights spilling from the gallery down the street and hear the distant sounds of voices and laughter.

She lingered in the gathering darkness, sorry she'd ever left the loft. The dark had chased her out. Now the dark again threatened to envelop her, here on this city street with its one lighted doorway. But inside were crowds, which she hated; even worse, they were crowds of strangers admiring other artists' work.

Feeling fragile and transparent as glass, Jamie gritted her teeth. She tucked her fine, pale hair back behind one ear and squared her shoulders. The hell with them! She'd go take a look, say hello to the few people she was bound to know, then go get a nice sweet cappuccino on the way home. Yes, that would be fine; she could do that. She'd make herself do that.

Just beyond the circle of light, a man stood alone, aloof and unapproachable. He looked away, disdainful of the noise billowing out of the gallery, the couples sauntering by arm in arm. He seemed to exist apart from it all, solitary, silent, and inscrutable. And then he saw her.

The woman had paused halfway up the block and stood, leaning slightly forward, her pale, ash-blond hair blowing about her face, her lips parted, her eyes wide. Lovely. So very lovely.

Like a knife, longing cut deep into his heart.

He'd never seen her before. She didn't look like someone he knew or had known in the past. He couldn't even see the color of her eyes. Yet there was something about her, something in the way she stood, in the faraway look on her face, in the way she lifted one hand to her cheek to brush the hair away, something that inexplicably took hold of him and shook him to his very soul.

This is why you're here tonight, a voice whispered in his head. *This is the reason.*

No, he thought, feeling afraid for the first time in years. No.

But he stood his ground. And as she approached he straightened, stiffened his shoulders, sucked in his breath. His hands curled into fists and he shoved them deep into his pockets. Watching, you would have thought he was preparing for battle.

But Jamie wasn't watching.

She was scouting out the situation, gathering her courage before stepping inside. She hesitated, one foot behind the other as she debated her next move.

"There's quite a crowd in there."

Jamie spun toward the voice and blinked. The man standing in the shadows was so handsome, it took her breath away. But she managed to find her voice. "Yes, there is. I can't quite decide whether to take the plunge."

"What are you looking for?"

"Pardon?"

"If you're here to see the photographs, they're interesting. Wonderful print quality and some evocative subjects. But you would enjoy them more on a quiet morning." He paused, his dark eyes narrowing. "If you're here to *be* seen . . ." He let his words drift into silence.

"I think I'll pass," Jamie said. She lifted her shoulders in a little shrug, reached up, and tucked her windblown hair behind one ear. "Well . . . thanks for the tip. Good night."

"Wait!" He stepped out of the shadows of the building, directly into her path. "Wait. Can I walk you home?"

Jamie made a small sound, half laughter, half disbelief. In this city? He had to be kidding . . . or crazy! "No," she said firmly. "But thank you anyway."

"Wait." He touched her arm, then quickly stuffed his hands back in his pockets. He was so handsome, so dark and intense that she felt hypnotized, a deer caught in oncoming headlights. She blinked up at him, motionless, waiting.

The expression on his face was at once eager and distant, a clash of contradictions. It depended where you looked, Jamie thought, whether you looked at the hard straight line of his beautiful mouth, or into those dark and burning eyes. She wavered between the two, sensing something she could feel but not name, an unspoken but tangible battle taking place in the darkness surrounding the two of them.

Then he leaned toward her, and for the craziest second she thought he was going to kiss her. Her heart raced, pounding against her ribs. Her eyes widened. But all he did was say something in a whisper.

"Pardon?" she asked, flustered and blushing. "I'm sorry; I didn't hear—"

"I said, you're safe here. There's got to be two hundred people not twenty feet away. Light. Noise. Stay for a minute." And then he added softly, "Please?"

"Why should I?"

"Because, surprisingly, I'm anxious to talk, to hear another voice. Because if you leave, I'll be forced back inside to all that frantic fun. I'll be forced to 'mingle.' " Eyes dark and serious, he still managed to imbue the word with great sarcasm.

It broke the tension strung tight between them. She laughed. "Oh no, a fate worse than death!"

"At times." He smiled, and it was like a light flicking on behind his eyes. Still dark as coals, mesmerizing, suddenly they had depth and warmth, mystery but a strange vulnerability as well.

Jamie shrugged. "Well, I guess I could stay for a moment—"

He held his hand out. "My name is Edward Rockford."

She took his hand, felt the strength in his grip, the coolness of his skin. Felt as though she had done this before, if only in a dream. It was as though she knew the feel of his hand; anticipated the tingle climbing the nerves of her arm; recognized the very touch of him somewhere deep within her being.

Then reality intervened. "I'm Jamie Payton," she said, quickly breaking the touch. "So," she countered, her voice almost challenging, "if you hate these things so much, what are you doing here?"

"I had this feeling—" He said without thinking, then caught himself. He shook his head, began again. "I came with some friends. It was their choice."

What had he wanted to say? Jamie wondered. What had he begun to say? But perhaps it was better not to know. Matching his coolness, she nodded.

"The same here. A friend—a neighbor really—gave me a ticket. But I wasn't sure I was going to come until the last minute. I was busy working."

"What do you do?"

"I paint."

"Do you? What kind of paintings?"

Jamie heard the words running between them like birds twittering in the air above, thin, light sounds calling back and forth, while somewhere on the horizon a storm loomed. The air grew dense and charged with electricity. There was the barely perceptible rumble of thunder, a vibration felt more than heard. Her skin pricked with warning, a mixture of fear and anticipation. With her mind she followed the light, easy chatter; her body, every nerve, every fiber, was tensed for the oncoming turbulence.

"Abstracts," she answered, without missing a beat. "Large canvases, in oil. Occasionally watercolor, but oil is really my medium."

"Are you represented in any of the galleries in town?"

"A few. I did have a show recently, but it wasn't very successful."

One dark brow rose, but his gaze never wavered. "Why did you tell me that?"

"Pardon?" she asked, wrapping her arms around herself and taking a step back.

Edward smiled. "Don't get nervous. I just wondered why you added the fact that the show didn't go well. Just having a show is quite an accomplishment. I would have been extremely impressed—"

"I couldn't care less whether you're impressed or not, Mr. Rockford."

"Obviously. But I am. And perhaps the fault lay with the audience and not the artist. Did you ever consider that possibility?"

She ducked her head. "Every time I start a new canvas," she admitted, letting a smile climb from her lips to her eyes. But then she looked away. "You know, I'd really better be going."

"Back to work so late at night? Couldn't I talk you into a late dinner? Coffee?"

"No. Thank you, but no."

"Why not?"

"Because I said so."

Edward gave a half nod of acquiescence and looked away, off into the brightly lit interior of the gallery. His profile was turned to her, immobile and proud, all hard lines and chiseled surfaces. Jamie had this strange, unexplainable urge to touch his face, to break that facade of control, to make him ask again. . . . Oh, she wanted him to ask again. It was crazy, but she did.

He glanced back at her, annoyance firing his dark gaze. "You're a problem, Ms. Payton. A dilemma upon whose horns I'm caught. On one hand, you've been quite honest, and obviously you have no interest in getting to know me further. You'd like me to go away. Disappear. But on the other hand"—he shrugged, his broad shoulders lifting within the smooth fabric of his suit jacket, the fabric shifting, sliding like a second skin he'd like to shed—"on the other hand, I have the strangest feeling that . . ."

Jamie held her breath, transfixed.

But he stopped. He narrowed his eyes, a wry grin tugging at the corner of his mouth. "Never mind," he finished coldly. "Even I wouldn't buy what I was going to say. Forget it."

Jamie let her breath out and felt her soul deflate. Sadness washed over her. Suddenly she was tired, just plain tired. She didn't know what was going on and didn't want to, didn't want to be feeling any of these strange and confusing feelings. She wanted to be home alone in her loft, dark or not.

She sighed. "Well, good night. Good-bye. It was nice meeting you."

"My pleasure," he answered.

She gave him a little smile, then settled the strap of her pocketbook more comfortably on her shoulder and shoved her hands in the pocket of her skirt. " 'Night."

"Can I get you a cab? I'd feel better knowing you were safe."

"Oh, it's not necessary. I walk all the time—"

"Please?" Without waiting, Edward strode to the curb and flagged a passing taxi. He held the door open for her, then reached in the front window and handed the driver a twenty. "She'll give you the address." He turned and smiled at her, their eyes locked in the silence for a moment, and then he stepped back. With one hand raised in farewell, he let the cab pull away.

Jamie turned in her seat, but already Edward Rockford was a distant shadowy figure, no more than a dream . . . and then he was gone. She bowed her head, rubbing at the pain throbbing above her eyes.

The cabdriver said, "Thought we were going to have a storm here for a while, but it seems to have passed us by."

Passed us by. The words seemed to be the saddest on earth, whispering of chances missed, hopes unfulfilled, dreams vanished like mist. And for the second time that week Jamie started to cry.

THREE

Jamie couldn't sleep. Moonlight poured in through the windows of the loft. Mysteries played in her mind.

She got out of bed, lit the candles, and sat straight-backed on the hard kitchen chair, uncomfortable and exhausted. How ridiculous to be sitting awake at two o'clock in the morning. And why? Because of a man, a handsome stranger who had appeared out of nowhere and disappeared as quickly? Yet even now she could feel the way her pulse had raced when he looked at her . . . just as she could feel a sharp stab of envy at the success of the photography show. She ducked her head. Oh, it was terrible to feel this way! She hated it, hated the wanting, the wishing. What did she think . . . that some good fairy was going to appear and grant her wish? That suddenly she'd find success and happiness? That crowds of people would flock to one of her shows, and that someone she loved would be there to share it with her? That magic was going to happen?

Filled with a strange restlessness, she walked over and leaned on the windowsill. But out there were only the stars, the universe all cold and distant, pinpoints of light in a dark sky. Panic fluttered in her chest and she clutched the windowsill, her eyes searching the night, seeking comfort, seeking something—

And there he was. She caught only a glimpse of him, tall and broad-shouldered, before he disappeared down the street and into the darkness. But he had been there. She was sure of that, and sure, also, that it was the man she had met earlier. Edward Rockford. Yes. She was as sure of it as she was of her own name.

And she wasn't frightened. Startled for the moment, yes, but not afraid. It was as if something deep inside her had expected him to appear almost magically, conjured up by that wild rush of longing and need she had felt. She could almost believe he was somehow connected to all the extraordinary things that had been happening to her: the strange little shop, the old man and his gift of paints, the unfinished canvas . . . all of it seemed linked in some unfathomable way. And he, Edward Rockford, was at the center of it all . . . the key to the mystery.

Jamie laughed out loud, shivering within the circle of her own arms. That's nonsense and you know it, Jamie Payton, she scolded herself. That could have been anyone: some guy heading home after his bowling league, a man out walking his dog. Anyone. You're acting crazy. Pull yourself together. Do something sensible.

And like a magnet, the painting pulled her.

Slipping a long cotton shirt on over her nightgown, she hurried to the easel and stood for a moment, studying the unfinished canvas. By candlelight the details were indistinct, but there was some really nice work there: depth and balance, a strong use of color . . . and that remarkable sense of light. Much better than usual, Payton, she thought, and reached for the box of paints.

Just touching them sent a powerful energy flowing up her arm. In her hand, the brush trembled. As before, images crowded into her head, unbidden but unstoppable: fragments of memories or wishes; faces glimpsed and forgotten or merely dreamed; places seen once long ago or longed for in reverie. Nothing real. Nothing she could name. But they were powerful and marvelous, and they filled her with a wild exuberance.

Jamie stood there in her nightgown and painted by candlelight, breaking all the rules of formal training and common sense. She wasn't aware of anything but the physical effort of putting brush to canvas. Nothing else penetrated the seamless cocoon of her concentration.

She stood there with one hip cocked, her painting arm thrust forward aggressively. She was breathing through parted lips, quickly, high in her throat. Her heart drummed. She didn't want to stop. She felt compelled, driven.

She worked for over two hours, until the windows turned gray with the first hint of morning light, until her eyelids grew heavy, until sleepiness overcame her sense of urgency. Washing out her brushes, she kept her back turned to the canvas, and she didn't look at it as she blew out the candles and fell into bed. It would be waiting for her, like a surprise, until the morning. It was a very exciting thought.

But if excitement was the feeling she fell asleep with, dismay greeted her when she woke up.

It *was* a landscape, no denying it now. There were high-shouldered hills carpeted in lush forest green, a winding road, a house.

Her mouth went dry.

It wasn't possible. She painted abstracts. Always had. Always would. Yet there it was, real as daylight. Mountainsides. Road. House. Even a door on the house.

She stepped back, frightened. She could shrug off exhausted fantasies in the middle of a sleepless night, but morning meant reality. Sanity. The world as she knew it. So there had to be some rational explanation for this, there just *had* to be!

But what?

If only there was someone she could show the painting to, maybe they could explain what was going on. Maybe she was just seeing things that weren't there. Maybe someone had been fooling with the painting while she slept—

Jamie stopped, angry suddenly, caught somewhere between disbelief and fear. She was tired of puzzles, of mysteries she couldn't solve. She wanted things back to normal. So to hell with it! She'd get rid of this canvas and start over.

Lifting the painting with both hands, she took it off the easel, leaned it against the wall, and put a fresh clean canvas in its place. But even that wasn't enough; the landscape drew her eyes, seemed to beckon. Roughly she stuck it behind a whole pile of canvases waiting to be discarded. There. Done. She'd paint with more control next time.

At seven that night there was a knock on her door. Jamie had been sitting and reading the newspaper, despairing over the civil wars raging in Eastern Europe, the violence and hunger in the cities. Gratefully, she tossed the paper aside and pulled open the door.

She honestly didn't know whether or not she was surprised.

"Hello. I hope I'm not disturbing you."

Edward Rockford stood there, broad-shouldered, dark-haired, unsmiling, holding flowers and a gold-foil-wrapped box of candy.

Jamie nodded. Then she stepped out into the hall and pulled the door shut behind her. "How did you find me?"

He shrugged. "J. Payton. You're listed in

the book." He paused, his dark eyes traveling over her face. "Do you mind?"

"I don't know," she answered, not bothering to be polite. "I don't know if I want to ask you in. I never do that kind of thing. Never. It's too dangerous."

"You're right. Never take chances." He said it with such intensity that Jamie finally had to smile.

"Well, it's not like I've made it my motto, like the golden rule or something. I just try to be careful, sensible."

"Good. Yes." He nodded, dark brows pulled low over his dark, gorgeous eyes. He glanced around, looking as if the narrow landing were a cage he was trapped in, and shrugged again. "Can I take you out to dinner? Somewhere public, safe. We can take a cab. I'll wait for you downstairs."

It didn't make a lick of sense, not a bit. But he was irresistible, standing there looking so handsome, so formal, yet so boyish in his nervousness.

"All right. I guess so. I'll be ready in ten minutes."

"Take your time. And these are for you. I . . ." He started to say something else, but bit back the words. Merely handed her the pink roses, the chocolates, and laid a hand on the banister. "I'll be waiting downstairs."

She closed the door behind her, locked it, and leaned back against it, holding the flowers in one hand, the candy in the other.

"This is unbelievable!" she whispered, her cheeks warm, her blood racing. She should just send him away. She should go downstairs and give him hell for bothering her. The nerve of the man after she'd told him no last night. She should make it clear that she meant what she said. But . . . did she? She bit her lip, unable to give a name to what she was feeling: flattered? enchanted? intrigued? No, it was far more than that, an attraction she couldn't understand or resist. There was no way she could keep herself from going down those stairs to him.

"I'm surprised you're here," he said with a smile that startled and delighted her. They sat across from each other at a linen-covered table in a quiet French restaurant.

"No more than I am," Jamie admitted with a wry little grin. She tipped up her chin. "What made you ask, then, if you were so sure I wouldn't accept?"

"I couldn't help myself." He said it lightly,

but his eyes betrayed him. With a shrug, he went on. "I had to see you again. I thought of tracking down the gallery that handles your paintings, buying one, then calling you. But I couldn't wait. I had to see you tonight. I . . . I can't explain it."

"Oh, that's explanation enough! It's a bit . . . I don't know, overwhelming, I guess. It makes me uncomfortable."

"I'm feeling a bit edgy myself."

And the truth was, Jamie could hear the tension in the breath he drew, could see the knotted muscles in his neck. Her own hands were clasped white-knuckled in her lap. She had to laugh, she couldn't help herself.

"We're quite a pair, you and me," she said, relaxing finally. She brushed the hair back from her face and rested a cheek in one hand, still smiling at him.

He leaned toward her. "You have a wonderful smile. And beautiful eyes."

"Me?" She laughed again, caught by surprise.

"Yes, you! Beautiful eyes, a gray like soft flannel, or a dove's breast. And flecked with gold like the sky right at dusk."

Jamie sat back, blushing furiously. She pressed her fingertips to her forehead, covering her face with the flat of one hand. "Stop. Enough."

"I'm sorry," Edward said quickly, touching her hand for a fleeting second, then taking hold of his glass as though he meant to crush it. "I'm sorry. Really. I won't . . . I didn't mean to embarrass you. I'll be careful."

And he was. Once they ordered, he talked about the weather, about D.C. in the summer, the latest performance at the Kennedy Center, about sailing on Chesapeake Bay. He sat slightly back from the table, his hand curled around the stem of his wineglass, his gaze directed somewhere just over her shoulder.

It suited Jamie just fine; it gave her a chance to study him boldly, without having to risk the same scrutiny from those dark, intense eyes. What she had taken as handsomeness was more than that. There was a brooding, intense sensuality to the man, a physical presence that was compelling, powerful. Broad-shouldered, he still gave the impression of a lean and supple grace. His hands were strong; she'd felt them at her elbow, holding her close beside him as they had walked the city streets, helping her in and out of the taxi on the way to the restaurant. But more often than not he pushed them deep in his pockets or sat as now, seemingly at ease but tensed, silent, restrained.

That was it, she realized with a sudden rush of insight. Over all the sexiness, the powerful sensuality, there was a restraint. A holding back. A dark and definite reserve. Why? Who was he? What had happened in his life to cloak him in this harsh restraint?

He caught her staring and the blood rose to his face.

Jamie couldn't believe she'd actually made him blush. "Sorry." She quickly lowered her eyes to her wineglass and took a sip. "This is delicious. I'm enjoying it."

"I'm glad."

Okay, she thought, we've gone from too much to too little. What we need here is something in between, something neutral, nonpersonal. What she expected was a return to the weather.

But the expected didn't happen. Instead, Edward held her glance and spread his hands out on the table in front of him. "What would you like to know about me, Jamie?"

As if he had read her mind.

Jamie started to hedge, but he came to her rescue immediately. "Please, ask. You must want to know *something* about me, as cautious as you are."

"Wait," she said in self-defense. "I'm not neurotic or anything. I just don't like to tempt fate."

"Neither do I."

"Well, good. That's one thing in our favor," she quipped, flashing a quick smile. "Okay, the truth is there's a lot I'd like to know. But I'll start off easy, I promise. For example, what do you do?"

He smiled. "A kind beginning. Okay. I work for one of the major cable networks. I'm VP of the International Division, which means I sell the rights to American programming overseas. Europe. Asia. The Middle East."

"Oh, the traveling must be wonderful."

"It suits me. When they hired me to create this division, I got to design my own job. I made sure it involved plenty of travel."

"Yes, I can understand. All those places, the people, their art and architecture. I'd find it fascinating!"

"Yes, you probably would."

"Don't you?" she asked, wide eyes on his face.

He shrugged. "Usually what I see is the inside of one boardroom or another, one five-star hotel or another. It all begins to look the same. But"—he leaned across the table, his dark eyes absolutely serious—"perhaps we could go together sometime."

Jamie waved away his words with a laugh. "I'll hold off on that, thanks! This is our first date. We may decide we have nothing in common, nor the slightest attraction to each other."

"I'm afraid that's no longer a possibility from my point of view." He said it softly, his eyes holding hers, his face open and unguarded for the moment.

No. Slow down, slow down . . . she wanted to say. Instead she swallowed. Nodded. "Thank you," she said softly. "So . . . tell me some more about yourself."

Again that second of hesitation. "Well, I'm thirty-six, single. I work long hours. I like my job. I also like the theater, ballet, opera, and college basketball. I—" He grinned suddenly, shrugging in that boyish way he had that completely disarmed her. "I don't know what else to tell you."

"Are you divorced? Separated?"

"No." He seemed to want to leave it at that, but she was leaning toward him, brows raised, waiting, so he added, "I've never been married."

And though she wanted to ask why not, she didn't . . . yet. Instead, her sense of fairness compelled her to offer something personal for what she'd been given. "Me neither. I . . . well, I guess I've always been too busy. Did I tell you I'm a painter? Yes, well it seems to occupy me completely. I can't find time or energy for anything else. Sometimes I think I eat, sleep, and drink painting." She was leaning forward as she spoke, resting her chin on one propped hand, talking quickly as she always did once she got started, and she looked up into his eyes . . . and lost her train of thought. "I . . . um . . . what was I saying?" she asked, covering her face with one hand, laughing. "Oh my, it must be the wine. Sorry."

"That's okay. You were telling me about your painting. What are you working on now?"

She hesitated, a shadow of a frown crossing her eyes. "Oh, that's enough about my painting. Give me a chance and I'll bore you to tears."

"I'm not bored. Not one bit. I enjoy listening to you. It's nice to hear someone talk about their work with so much passion."

"Too much! I go on and on!" She groaned, frowning down at the tablecloth, at her own silliness.

"And who told you that lie?"

She looked up, startled beyond words. If she could have found her voice, she would have whispered, "My father. All my life, my father did." But luckily, by the time she could speak, she had herself back under control.

"Thanks," she said softly. "That was a nice comeback." With a smile rising to her eyes, she asked, "Are you that nice a person?"

"I've been called better—and worse. You'll have to find out for yourself."

"Maybe I'll do just that," she replied, empowered by a sudden rush of bravado.

And then, without planning it, she smiled right into his eyes. He made her feel good. Really good. He made her feel sexy and desirable, fascinating and irresistible. It was the way he watched her as she spoke, his complete and undivided attention. It was the look in his dark eyes, his interest, his admiration. All of it was going straight to her head, like a good stiff drink.

And he seemed to feel it, too. For just a second that reserve of his, that restraint, seemed to slip away, and she caught a glimpse of a different Edward Rockford, someone free and impetuous, passionate, someone imbued with more than a touch of wildness.

For a second their eyes locked and something traveled between them, touched and connected.

But it was too soon. Too scary.

Jamie laughed nervously and looked away, searching for the waiter, the maître d', *someone*!

"I'd kill for some more of that wonderful bread!" she quipped, leaning back in her chair. "Ummm . . . good crusty French bread and real butter. Sometimes I think I could live on that. And cheese! Though I know it's not good for you, the cheese and butter, I mean, but the taste! Oh, the pleasure is worth the penalty, don't you think?"

"I do," he agreed seriously, but there was the sound of laughter in his voice, a warm, intoxicating appreciation.

He had settled back, one arm leaned across the back of his chair, his head tipped back so that he was watching her from under his dark brows, dark lashes, his dark eyes focused on her face. The corner of his mouth tugged up in a smile. She could see his chest rise and fall with his breathing, see the smooth, tanned skin at his throat, the strong, elegant line of his jaw.

A giddy desire took hold of Jamie. She wanted to reach out, right across the table, right here, right now, and touch him. Needed to. Yearned to. Suddenly she had to know the feel of his skin, the feel of the bone beneath the skin, the shape and angle of his jaw, his cheek, his face . . . the roughness of that hint of a dark beard, the smoothness of his cheek and brow, the brush of his dark thick hair beneath her palm. It was like a fever, a sudden burning along her nerves, a strange and unfamiliar compulsion.

She clasped her hands in her lap and locked them between her knees.

At that moment Edward leaned across the table, stretched a hand out past the boundary of bread dish, water glass, candle. . . .

Jamie felt her heart bang against her ribs, pounding, pounding.

And then it was all over, or only imagined.

He picked up his water glass, took a drink, set it down.

The waiter appeared out of nowhere and poured coffee, offered dessert.

Jamie demurred. Food was not what she craved now. Tongue, lips, her whole *body* was riven with this strange, fierce desire. But not chocolate mousse . . . not crème brûlée. What she wanted was a taste of him . . . hot, hard, powerful, delicious. A forbidden taste. A wild embrace, a hot, wet kiss. A moment of utter and complete abandon! Now. This minute. She wouldn't wait, couldn't wait an instant longer.

And she knew he felt the same way. She could see the sweat of desire sitting on his skin, could see the unbearable yearning in his eyes, could almost feel the heat radiating from his body. A touch with her fingertip would sizzle; it would sear him, brand him with her mark forever. All she had to do was reach across this little space and touch him. He'd respond. He'd leap from his chair and take her in his arms—

"Shall we go?"

Jamie caught her breath. She blinked and the room swam back into focus. "Pardon?" she whispered, licking at dry lips.

He was leaning away, his brow furrowed over hooded eyes. "I was just wondering if you were ready to leave."

"Yes, of course."

He offered his hand as he pulled back her chair. "Would you like to go somewhere else? Have a drink? Listen to some music? Or shall I take you home?"

Jamie felt disoriented, and depressed. It was all just her imagining, her stupid fantasizing. Actually, it didn't seem to matter to him one way or the other: come, go . . . what the hell? He was probably bored, probably eager to go back to wherever and whatever his life really was. And she was also. Yes. This was crazy, ridiculous. She didn't want his attention, hadn't asked for it. The truth was, she had never wanted to get involved with this man in the first place. She might as well set him straight right now.

"Perhaps I'd better get home. There are things I need to do, and tomorrow . . . well, I've got to get to work early."

Edward looked at her a moment before he answered. But when he did speak, his voice was absolutely expressionless. "All right. I'll get us a cab."

They rode back in silence.

At her door he waited till she had the key turned in the lock.

"Good night, Jamie."

She pushed the door open and stepped inside. "Good night. I had a nice time. And"—she stuck her hand way out, straight from the shoulder—"it was nice meeting you, Edward. Perhaps we'll see each other again sometime."

He took her hand and held it, gently but firmly, his fingers wrapped around hers. He didn't say anything, just held her hand, held it tightly, the warmth traveling from his palm to hers, up her wrist, up her arm, filling her chest, and wrapping itself around her heart so that she felt an ache there, a strange yearning. Oh God, not again, she breathed. And still he held her hand and looked into her eyes. But then he let go.

"Good night, then. You're all right going in by yourself?"

"Of course."

"Do you want to turn on the lights first?"

"Sure," she said, flicking the switch. The lights came on, filling the loft with an ordinary electric glow.

"There. Everything's right as rain," she said, her words mocking her hidden feelings. "So . . . good night."

"Good night." He turned away, reaching for the banister, almost hurrying now.

Thin-lipped, frowning, she started to shut the door, sure, even as she did, that he was going to stop her, put a hand on the doorframe, a foot in the door. She thought so even as the lock clicked into place with a small metallic snap.

FOUR

Edward stopped at the foot of the stairs and leaned his head against the cool cinderblock wall. He shut his eyes and fought for control. *Be calm. Be ice.*

He commanded his body to obey his will: his blood to stop racing through his veins, his muscles to stop their sharp, eager aching, that ache of desire that had spread like fire across his shoulders and down his arms. Oh, how desperately he had wanted to touch her, to take her in his arms and feel the realness of her, the smoothness of her skin, the warmth of her breath against his cheek, the press of her breasts against his chest.

Now all he could do was endure the pain.

She had said good night. That was all. And

that was all he wanted, all he could afford to want. There was no denying the physical attraction between them; it was incredibly powerful. But there was something else, something he couldn't name that was drawing him to her, drawing him deeper and deeper into the unknown, tugging at him like a whirlpool at a swimmer's feet. He had to fight against it. He had to keep his balance. He couldn't let himself go too far.

All it took was control.

With control came distance and a life without complications or pain. It was the only sane thing to want in this world. He had learned that the hard way and he was far too smart to make the same mistake twice. Never. Not him. He would not charm her, dazzle her, sweep her off her feet. Not her, not this time. He would be careful, restrained, reticent even. Being alone was fine. It was enough.

But tonight it hurt, just as her prettiness hurt: her wide gray eyes lit with excitement when she talked, her smile, her laughter. The way she played with the smooth fall of pale hair that ended just at the curve of her chin. The way she tucked it behind one ear when she was thinking, that faraway look in her eyes.

Standing here alone, he could remember her every gesture, every tone of voice. And that sudden shyness—that reserve—that was deep at the heart of her like a grain of sand at the heart of a pearl. What was that all about? Had someone hurt her, wounded her? Is that why she was always on her guard?

Anger swept over him, along with a fierce need to protect her. Hundreds of years ago he would have donned his armor, mounted his steed, and ridden off to joust with his rival; he would have been her champion, her knight in shining armor. A hundred years ago he would have strapped on his six-guns, leaped on his horse, and raced off to the showdown. Ten years ago he would have raced back up these steps, pounded on her door, swept her off her feet and into his arms. Ten years ago . . .

But not now. No. Now he knew better and he would hold himself in check, hold back, be sane.

Then why did he feel like he was going crazy? He was shaking again, sweat standing out along his upper lip and across his brow. Wiping his face with one hand, he grabbed hold of the doorknob with the other and stepped out into the night air. There was music in the street, a crowd of people, cars honking and braking, voices calling from open windows.

Was it her voice, calling to him? As much as he might wish it, the answer was no.

Jaw clenched, eyes narrowed, he strode home without looking back.

FIVE

Days passed in Jamie's loft. The foil-wrapped box of candy sat untouched among turpentine rags and unopened mail. The pink roses wilted, their heavy heads drooping but giving off a sweet and delicate perfume. The scent of pink roses filled the loft. At times Jamie blamed that for her inability to paint. Like too much heat, or the sun shining in at the wrong angle, the sweet smell of the roses distracted her. Not a single one of the new paintings was any good. She tossed them away, but she couldn't make herself throw away the pink roses . . . nor would she touch the unfinished landscape.

Nights passed. Her sleep was filled with strange and unexplainable dreams. It was as though, because she refused to work on *that* painting, the disavowed landscape invaded her sleep. There were the hills, the trees, the road, and the house. And in the house someone waited. She could sense that person's waiting presence. Who? Who watched like that? Who waited?

And then a recurring nightmare came to her. She was a little girl again, locked in the back of a long black car, and her parents were walking away down a crowded street. She pulled and pulled on the door handles, banged and banged on the windows, and cried out their names, but they never even turned around. Other people stopped and stared, scolding her in loud angry voices: Be quiet! Stop making such a fuss. What a bad little girl!

She woke up crying, her pillow wet, her chest crushed with the weight of sorrow. She leaped out of bed and tried to get busy, fussing around the loft, tidying up, but all the time she was wishing she had a best friend to call and talk to, a buddy, a pal who would listen or, better yet, rush over to hold her hand, hold her close, hold her tight and safe against all the world. She needed somebody. And she hated herself for needing, hated her heart for aching, her lips for quivering, her hands for shaking. She hated her thoughts that turned relentlessly, uncontrollably, to a dark broad-shouldered man with smoldering eyes.

And then came her father's voice: *I told you, didn't I? Need no one. Depend on no one. Be someone to whom other people have to come crawling. Stop wasting your time with this ridiculous painting of yours. Stop being a nothing, a nobody—*

Jamie ran from the loft.

She fled down the stairs and out into the sunshine of a summer morning. The only place she could think of to go was the corner restaurant, and she sat there drinking coffee and nibbling on toast until the demons drew back into their hiding places.

Jamie took the long way home, stopping at the supermarket first, and she was panting by the time she climbed the last flight of stairs to the loft. Her arms were killing her; the two grocery bags seemed to have gained at least ten pounds each on the walk home. All she wanted to do was drop them on the floor outside her door, find her key, and stumble inside. It had been one hell of a morning.

As her foot touched the top landing someone reached out and lifted the bags from her arms. The sudden lightness made her feel as if she had sprouted wings and could fly away.

"Good morning," Edward said, his eyes

meeting hers over the tops of celery and whole-wheat bread.

"Edward! What are you doing here?" She was too startled to be subtle, too surprisingly happy.

"I called, but you didn't answer. I figured you were out, but then I regretted not walking you in the other night, not making sure you were safe. I didn't mean to intrude—"

"You're not," she said, suddenly giddy with pleasure. She didn't even stop to think. Flinging the door wide, she slipped behind him, put both hands flat against his broad back, and pushed him inside. "Can I make you breakfast? Lunch? It's not often that this cupboard's full. I've got fresh coffee beans here, and English muffins, cheese—"

Excitement seemed to leap from her to him like a charge of electricity, sparkling and crackling in the air between them. He broke into a grin. "Don't fuss. I'll take you out. Somewhere wonderful. Somewhere you've never been before. Name the one place you've always wanted to go and it's yours. Anywhere!"

"Tahiti," she answered, her eyes shining with laughter.

"All right," he said softly, "Tahiti it is."

He was smiling at her and there was a look

on his face, a contentment that softened his chiseled features and made him look breathtakingly young and handsome. The artist in her yearned to paint him, to catch that fleeting look. The woman in her just wanted to touch him. So she did.

He stiffened at the brush of her fingertips against his cheek, half closed his eyes, and held his breath. Then he closed the space between them and took her in his arms. Her hands circled his neck as she lifted onto tiptoe to fit herself against him.

And then he kissed her. His mouth was warm and sweet, hungry but gentle, his lips brushing across hers lightly at first. A low, rough groan rose in his throat and then he was kissing her passionately, his mouth pressing and turning and pressing against hers, tasting her sweetness, drinking it in, drawing it into his soul like a man who has been dying of thirst and finds himself at a sweet, fresh spring.

His passion awoke something within her. For the first time, the very first time, she felt as though kissing were everything. As though she could stand and kiss and be kissed, her weight leaning against his strength, her body pressed to his warmth, her head tipped back, her mouth open to his, forever.

From her toes to her fingertips, she felt alive, aware, sensitive to every move of his muscles, every intake of his breath, every point of contact between the two of them.

The two of them. It seemed incomprehensible. Crazy. Yet right in a way that nothing had ever felt right before. Look how they fit together. Look how he knew how much she needed to be kissed, to be held, to be caressed. He knew all about her, everything, without being told, as if he were a part of her, connected to her . . . as if this were meant to be, had *always* been meant to be, and she had been moving toward this all her life without ever knowing it.

There were tears brimming in her eyes when he lifted his head and looked down into her face.

"What? What is wrong, my darling?"

"Nothing," she said, blinking the tears away as she reached up and stroked his cheek. "Nothing is wrong. Everything feels right. I can't explain it—"

"Don't. Don't even try. Not now, not yet. Let me just hold you, look at you. You are so beautiful!" he whispered.

She pressed her forehead to his chest. "Oh, I'm not! But I'm glad you think so."

"I do," he breathed, kissing her lightly on

the top of her head, then tipping her face up so he could kiss her nose, her lips, her chin. "I do, I do."

She raked her fingers back through his hair, locked them behind his head, and drew his mouth back to hers.

She would kiss him without thought, without question. She would kiss him just the way she wanted to, all daring and teasing, running her tongue across his lips, probing the sweet interior of his mouth, luring his tongue into hers, kissing him fiercely, then softly, brazenly, then tenderly. She would let herself swoon here in his arms, drift, float, soar like a bird, drop like a stone so that he had to hold her weight in his arms like this, just like this. . . .

Edward felt her droop against him as if her very bones had melted, as if all the strength and icy resolve that held her together had turned to sugar water in the heat of their embrace. Tightening his arms around her narrow back, he pressed her to his chest. The feel of her breasts against his chest brought pain, a pang of longing and loss, of excitement and fear. It had been ten years since the feel of a woman in his arms had moved him this way. It meant nothing usually, nothing. Now it was like having his chest torn open, his heart ripped out.

He broke from their kiss, burying his face in the silk of her hair. His breath was harsh and ragged; his hands shook. He tried to turn away, to catch his breath, but she clung to him.

"Wait, darling. Wait, Jamie . . . just wait a minute—" He pulled away, moving out of her reach, his back turned. His arms were crossed in front of him, his shoulders hunched. His breathing made a harsh, frightening sound in the silent loft.

Jamie touched his shoulder.

Edward straightened, squaring his shoulders. He turned and smiled at her, touched her cheek, but there was a darkness behind his eyes and his hand lingered for only a moment before he moved away, talking as he reached for one of the shopping bags.

"Anything in here you have to put away before we go for lunch?"

"Nothing," she answered, trying to read his face, her gaze fastened there with a desperate intensity. Desire made her bold. "Are you all right? Edward? Will you talk to me . . . ?"

"Sure. What do you want to talk about?" he answered, cool and smiling. He leaned back against the wall, arms crossed lightly over his chest.

For Jamie, everything grew fuzzy, indistinct. Had she imagined the passion in their kiss? Had she imagined the pain she'd sensed within him? What was going on? What on earth was happening?

"Well, what do you want to talk about, Jamie Payton? Shall I tell you I'm glad to see you? As I said, I regretted not walking you in the other night."

"I was fine. I come in alone every night," she replied, trying to focus on his words. She felt so strange: caught between two realities, or reality and fantasy. Trapped in the Twilight Zone! The idea made her laugh.

He looked at her, dark eyes narrowed, puzzled. "What's so funny?"

"Nothing." She shrugged, shaking her head. "Everything. It doesn't matter. Listen." She cocked one hip suggestively. "Are you taking me to lunch or not? I've got a dozen things I should be doing—"

"None as important . . . or pleasant, I hope . . . as lunch with me," he answered, matching her bantering tone.

She smiled up at him, about to give some clever reply, but real emotion filled her chest. Her smile wobbled. When he stood this close, crazy feelings welled up from some unknown place. Hopes. Wishes. She just couldn't deal with it. She didn't *want* to deal with it!

"Jamie?" His voice was low and rough-edged. He bent toward her, reached for her.

But she was not having any of it, damn him. Keep it light. Keep it cool. If he could do it, so could she!

Pushing him away with the flat of one hand, as if she were still teasing, she busied herself with the groceries. "I think I'm in the mood for a picnic. I'll make some peanut-butter-and-jelly sandwiches and we'll find a park or somewhere. The sun is shining. No clouds. How's that sound to you?"

One dark brow rose in surprise. "But I promised you lunch."

"No, you promised me Tahiti," she answered. "But I've never put much faith in promises."

Edward tried to take her hand as they walked through Georgetown, but Jamie held tightly to the handle of the basket she was carrying and swung it back and forth, keeping a space between them.

He gave up and shoved his hands in his

pockets. "You look like Little Red Riding Hood," he said, sliding a glance her way.

"Well, that makes you either the Big Bad Wolf . . . or the Brave Huntsman."

"Which would you prefer?"

She shook her head. "I don't want either. I've had enough of wolves, and I don't want to be in need of rescue, thank you. No. What I'd like to do is rewrite the fairy tale."

"All right, then that's what we'll do," he said seriously, his gaze resting full on her face.

"Who are you?" Jamie demanded, coming to an abrupt halt.

He laughed sharply. "What does that mean?"

"I mean the truth. Who are you, Edward? What do you want with me?" Her wide eyes were troubled, searching. "Where did you come from? How did you happen to be there, at that gallery that night? At my door? Are you really interested in getting to know me? Because I am tired of playing games."

"I'm more than interested in you, Jamie Payton," he said, taking hold of her shoulders and leaning toward her. "I'm drawn to you. I'm desperate to know you. Don't you feel it? Can't you see I'm helpless to stay away? God knows I tried. I did. But here I am—" He flung his hands wide, then let them drop to his sides. His face was a mixture of longing and despair.

But Jamie was not going to make this easy. "Why?" she demanded. "Why are you, as you say, drawn to me? And why does that make you so unhappy?"

"Unhappy?" With a harsh laugh Edward turned and stalked a dozen yards away, then strode back. "Unhappy? Try frightened to death. Try terror-stricken. Try"—he looked at her, his eyes filled with passion— "try happier than I have been in more years than I care to remember. Burning, breathless . . . blessed." He said the last in a whisper, his face close to hers. "Oh, Jamie, I don't understand it. I can't explain it. I won't even try to give a name to whatever brought us together on that sidewalk that night." He shook his head slowly, his gaze so deep and open she could see into his soul. "All I know is that I feel something, something unhoped for—"

He shrugged, struggling to find the word that would explain, yet not sound crazy, even to himself. He couldn't. "Won't you help me? Tell me what you think. Say something."

She backed away from him, beyond the reach of his hands. This was more than she had bargained for. Shaking her head, she whispered, "I don't know what to say. I . . .

I *really* don't think I want to deal with this, Edward. You don't understand."

"Help me understand."

"I can't. I can't figure it out myself. All I know is that I don't want to deal with any of this. Strange things have been happening, and I just want them to stop. My painting . . . dreams . . . you. All of it is too much."

"Too much?"

"Too much to deal with. Too much to bear."

"Too much to bear?" he echoed, his piercing gaze cutting right to the heart of her. "Interesting, isn't it, Jamie, how carefully we both avoid the truth. No, don't turn away. You know what I mean! I say I haven't felt anything for ten years, and you don't ask why not. *You* . . . No, listen to me! . . . *You* pull away from my touch, from any mention of love . . . and *I* don't ask why. Too much to bear, Jamie Payton? We're both carrying things locked inside us that seem unbearable, but we go on, you and I, don't we? We deal with it. But happiness, the possibility of happiness . . . *that* scares the hell out of us."

"*You* scare the hell out of me, Edward. You! Standing here and talking in riddles. We were going for a damn picnic, and instead we're standing on some street corner and arguing. I don't need this. And I certainly don't feel like a picnic. I'm going home."

"Back to hide in your loft?"

"Damn you, Edward! Just leave me alone. Take this—" She threw the basket down at his feet. "Find someone else to picnic with and just leave me alone!"

As he bent to pick up the basket Jamie took off at a run and disappeared down the street.

Clenching his jaw, ignoring the stares directed his way, Edward stuffed the food back in the basket, then stood, tall and imperious. There to his left, behind a low stone wall, was an old church. Stepping over the wall, he walked up the path and set the basket just inside the church door. A bronze plaque caught his eye. DEDICATED TO ST. JUDE, PATRON SAINT OF DESPERATE SITUATIONS.

Wouldn't you know it? He laughed, the bitterness of the sound making an old parishioner turn and stare. With a rough shove, Edward pushed the door open and was gone.

Back in the loft Jamie gathered up the pink roses and threw them in the trash, leaving a trail of bruised petals across the wooden floor.

SIX

"Look at this," Jamie commanded, propping her painting, *the* painting, against the wall in front of Karl Viereck. Viereck had sponsored her first show and many of her larger canvases still hung along one wall of his gallery. She had her back to them now, and again she pointed at the unfinished painting she had carried in.

"So, what do you think? Is it garbage, a piece of junk?"

"Interesting way to present a work of art . . . especially your own," Karl commented with amusement, "but then you have never been much of a saleswoman." He wiggled his brows at Jamie, then turned his attention to the painting, squinting, stepping back, squinting some more, stepping up close. "You painted this?"

"Yes." She nodded, holding her breath. "Why? Does it look different to you?"

He leaned back on his heels, pursed his lips. "Well, now that I look carefully, I can see that it's your painting certainly; your brushwork, your use of color. But—"

"But . . . ?" she prompted, needing to hear him say it, needing to hear someone say: "My goodness, Jamie Payton, you painted a landscape. Now that's a surprise!" So *say* it, she thought; say it and save my sanity, what little is left. "But what? Tell me."

He cast her a sideways, skeptical look. "What I see here is not your usual work. There is something much more emotional here, something to do with the light you've captured, something—"

"What?" she prompted again, knowing what he was about to say.

He grinned at her. "I was going to say, there is something almost 'mystical' about this painting, but I know how you dislike that kind of thing."

"Oh." She sighed, totally bewildered now. "That's all?"

"That's all?" he repeated, mocking her. "Jamie, if you had painted me a dozen paintings like this one, with this kind of power and intensity, this emotional impact, I could have sold them all."

"Oh."

"Oh? I'm telling you that you have hit upon something, some energy, some vision in your work that can make all the difference in your career. And you say 'oh'? Are you all right?"

"I'm fine. I think." She shrugged. "It's strange—"

"Yes, it is."

"No, I meant, it's strange how I see this painting. It's driving me crazy because *I* see—" She stopped, feeling foolish. She had to bite back an awkward grin. "I see something inside the painting, something else."

Karl looked at her with concern. "And what do you see, Jamie?"

His perusal flustered her. She hated to be stared at. With a wave of her hand, she tried to change the subject. "Nothing. It's silly. Forget I said anything." She bent down and lifted the painting off the floor, then began to rewrap it in brown paper. "Gee, I always forget how heavy this is. Here, could you hold it for me a second, please, Karl?"

"Certainly." He held it between his hands while she looped twine around it. His fingers tightened on the package. He frowned. "Perhaps you'd like to leave it with me, Jamie. I have a feeling that a customer might find it irresistible."

"But it isn't finished."

"It's very beautiful!"

"But it isn't finished, Karl." Jamie laughed, taking the package from his hands and holding it to her chest.

"Then promise me that you'll work on it soon, and bring it back the moment it's done."

"Of course I will." She shrugged. "You handle all my work."

"But I want this one, Jamie, and I want it soon."

"Sure. Fine," she said, backing toward the door. "I'll see you, Karl. And thanks."

"My pleasure. And Jamie . . . ? Get something to eat. You look pale and tired."

"I will not. I shall not. I won't. I shan't." Jamie repeated the words over and over again like a litany. She would not work on *that* painting.

She had been at the easel since midafternoon, trying canvas after canvas, even resorting to old art-studio exercises to get her creativity flowing. Nothing worked. The whole day had been a big failure.

Now, at midnight, she had the oilcloth pinned over the windows. The box of paints from the little store was lying open and ready on the table. And her painting, the mysterious landscape, was on her easel . . . waiting.

The moment she picked up her brush, touched its tip to the paint, and laid it on that canvas, all her resistance disappeared. A sense of rightness filled her. It was like music. Like good wine. Like happiness. It flooded her, washing away the fear, the anger, the grief . . . washing it all away and filling her instead with joy and power.

She let the paint take her. She gave herself up to the flow of color, the mysterious images in her mind, the overwhelming passion of painting. She didn't think. She didn't interpret. She didn't even worry about it. She just painted until she couldn't stand.

And then she dropped into bed and slept like a baby.

SEVEN

In her sleep, Jamie heard the knock on the door.

It slipped into her dream, a new and wonderful dream in which she floated above forest-clad hillsides, the sun warm on her back as she glided sweetly, steadily home. It was a feeling she had never had before. Below, in that house, someone who loved her was waiting. There, at the door. She could almost see him—

The knock came louder this time, waking her. And there was a voice to go with it.

Her eyes popped open. Sitting up, she ran a hand through her hair and rubbed her eyes.

"Jamie?" It was a man's voice, low but insistent. *His* voice.

She considered not answering. She'd sit

here, silent, ignoring him, until he went away. She even leaned back against the wall and folded her arms across her chest in preparation for the siege. But some irresistible yearning betrayed her.

"Who's there?" she called.

"It's me . . . Edward Rockford." A pause. "Please, Jamie, give me just a minute to explain."

"Ha!" she snorted, good and mad already, remembering their sidewalk argument. "Go away."

She listened for the sound of his retreating footsteps but the silence was absolute. Nothing, no one moved.

"Well," she demanded, raising her voice, "are you gone yet? I'm busy. I've got work to do and no time to waste. I think you should just go away."

She waited again, leaning forward to listen better, straining to hear. Nothing.

"Have you gone?"

"No."

It almost made her smile. Straightening up, she clenched her jaw and narrowed her eyes. Let him stand there, then, till he grew roots.

Nursing her anger, she got out of bed, went in and washed her face, brushed her teeth, tucked her nightgown in the drawer, and slipped into jeans and a T-shirt. She straightened the sheets and folded the sleeper sofa. She went into the little kitchen alcove and got her coffee beans out of the freezer.

Then she stopped, listening. Nothing.

She pressed the top of the grinder and noise filled the loft along with the rich, dark smell of fresh-ground coffee. She set in the filter, poured in the water, got out her favorite mug.

"Well . . . ?" she called. "Have you left yet?"

Not a sound.

She stepped firmly to the door, unlocked it, and looked outside. "Oh, so you're still here. Well, I'm just getting my newspaper—"

Edward bent and handed it to her, but he wouldn't let go. Jamie lifted one brow and shrugged. She put both hands on her hips. "Keep it, then. I really don't care." And she turned to go back inside.

"Jamie. May I come in? Please? For a moment only."

"I *don't* think so." She met his eyes, those dark eyes, those stormy, turbulent eyes that drew her in, deeper and deeper—

"Come in, then," she grumbled. "But only for a minute."

"Thank you."

"Don't thank me. I don't intend to make this pleasant." She poured herself a mug of coffee, sat on the only chair, and propped her chin in her palm. "So?"

Edward stood in the center of the room, his hands shoved deep in the pockets of his dark slacks, wearing a pale blue shirt open at the neck, the sleeves rolled up over his forearms. "I'm not here to apologize—" he began, but Jamie cut him short.

"Then you might as well leave." She put her mug down and faced him straight on, both palms set square on her knees.

A wry half smile twisted his lips. He drew a deep breath. "All right, then, I apologize. But I would also like to explain."

"What?"

"About the other day. About the things I said—"

"I told you then, Edward, I don't think I want to pursue this."

"Why not? What? Were you going to say you don't care? Is that going to be your answer?"

"I don't have to answer, not to you or anyone else. I am my own person. Grown-up, independent, answerable only to myself."

"Which would be wonderful . . . if you were happy."

"I *am* happy! How dare you? How dare you tell me what I'm feeling? What do you think you are, a fortune-teller? A mind reader?"

"I'm just a man, a man who happens to—" He stopped, breathing hard as though he had come to a dangerous place and was teetering there, balanced at the precipice. One more step and . . .

"Could I have a cup of coffee, please, Jamie?"

"No," she said.

"Jamie! Don't you hear me? Can't you see how hard this is for me?"

"Then go away. Go home, Edward—"

"I can't. I won't. I've spent ten years practicing not to feel anything. To be impervious to tenderness, caring . . . love. I've gotten very good at it. Sometimes I can even fool myself. I look in the mirror and the man looking back is cold and hard as granite. Nothing can touch me. Nothing can hurt me. Most certainly, nothing can reach inside me. But you did, Jamie. You did."

His eyes softened and a pleading vulnerability shone through before he dropped his gaze. But still, his voice shook. "Jamie, the night we met? I was not going to go out. I'd had it. Too many parties, too much meaningless socializing. I didn't want to go. But something drew me. Oh, don't look at me like that! I'm not saying there was some supernatural force—"

"Oh, good," Jamie answered with a nervous little laugh. "I was really going to worry about you."

"I've felt the same way lately, believe me." He grinned, holding her cautious gaze. "Jamie, maybe it was nothing more than my own unbeatable hope, my own foolish optimism, but I felt that I had to go that night. And when I saw you walking toward me, a voice in my head said, 'Yes, yes! This is what you've been waiting for.' Maybe it was just how beautiful you are, or maybe the way you hesitated, brushing the hair back from your face. But my . . . my heart seemed to know you."

Jamie drew back. "Maybe I only reminded you of whatever happened ten years ago—"

"No!" he said harshly, then lowered his voice and repeated the word, his eyes on her face. "No. Later, after the cab had pulled away, I thought about that too. I tried to make that the reason; it would have explained it all so simply." His beautiful mouth curved in a wry grin. "And then perhaps I could have forgotten you. But no, Jamie, no such luck."

She grinned back, the corners of her lips pulled down. She was feeling the same warring emotions as he, the same bewilderment, the same irresistible attraction. "Do you want milk in your coffee? Sugar?" she asked with a forlorn sigh.

"No, just black, thanks . . . honey," he teased.

They both laughed. Jamie poured a mugful and brought it back to him, then sank onto the couch next to him. She touched his free hand, lightly, then folded her hands in her lap. "Edward? What happened ten years ago? Would you tell me now?"

He bowed his head over his coffee mug, and for a moment he seemed lost to her, staring down into the dark liquid. Then he lifted his head and met her eyes. "I was wild. Brash. So damn sure of myself. I fell in love with a girl. She was in love with me. I . . . I talked her into eloping. It sounded daring. Thumb your nose at tradition, that kind of thing. She was from a big midwestern family and she wanted a bridal party, a rehearsal dinner . . . all of it. I made it a test of her love. Come run off with me. Do it! The hell with everything else—" He swallowed around the lump in his throat, trying unsuccessfully to catch his breath, smooth the anguish out of his voice. "There was an accident on the way. A drunk driver. She was killed."

"Oh, Edward—" Jamie whispered, the tears sliding down her cheeks. "Oh, I am so sorry. So, so sorry . . ." She touched his arm, rested a cheek against his shoulder. She wanted to throw her arms around him, hug him to her breast, hold him so tight he wouldn't shake like that, but all she could do was pat his hand.

He let his head drop back on the couch, kept his eyes closed. The muscles along his jaw bunched and jumped, but he kept his teeth clenched. He didn't make a sound. After a while he lifted his head, wiped at his face with one hand, and took a sip of cold coffee.

"Sorry," he said softly. "I'm sorry. It's the first time I've spoken that aloud."

"Oh, Edward . . ." She bit her lips. "I just wish there was something I could do or say. I am so sorry. I shouldn't have made you talk about it."

"I had to talk about it! Don't you see, Jamie?" he said, turning to face her, his knees touching hers, making him real, solid, a presence she couldn't ignore. "All the tricks I've used for years don't work anymore. And it's because of you. Because, like it or not, *want* to or not, I'm feeling things again. My defenses are shot. I couldn't keep up the facade any longer. I couldn't go on that way."

"But then what do we do? I don't know what else to do. I don't know how else to be."

He pulled her close, so close that he could feel the swift, light flutter of her heart against his chest. He closed his eyes, pressed his face to her hair. "I don't know either, my darling. All I know is that holding you like this seems to be its own answer." He buried his face in her hair, breathing in her scent, feeling the warmth of her, drawing it into him to warm him, revive him. That sweet warmth could fill all the emptiness inside him.

But she pulled away. "Edward, don't hold me so tightly."

"Why?" he asked, hurt and confused.

Jamie shook her head and slid away. "I don't know. It . . . it makes me uncomfortable. I . . . I don't know. I just—"

"Do you have any feelings for me?" he asked, leaning back as coolly as if he were asking about the weather.

"Feelings for you?" she repeated foolishly, blinking hard.

"Yes, Jamie. Feelings. Desire? Passion? A trace of love?"

"Edward, I told you from the very start that I wasn't looking to get involved. I'm so busy. I'm so wrapped up in—"

"I know," he snapped. "Wrapped up in your painting. Yes. I know how important that is to you. Something you can do all by yourself. Alone. Isolated. Something you can do and then beat yourself up about. The paintings aren't good enough. They didn't sell well at the show. They—"

"You don't know anything about it. That just proves how little you know about me, how little you understand. I love painting."

"It makes you happy?"

"Of course it makes me happy!"

"Then you're happy now. Happy with your life exactly as it is and I'm just an unwanted intrusion."

"I didn't say that."

"Then what did you say?" he asked softly, leaning toward her so that his breath was warm on her face, his eyes searching hers. "What do you want to say, Jamie?"

"I don't know," she whispered, trying to look away. But he took hold of her chin and gently turned her face back to his.

"Tell me, Jamie. What have you always wanted to tell, but there's no one to tell it to? What have you needed to share, what joys, what tears, and not had a shoulder to cry on?" He slid an arm around her and pulled her close against his side. "Tell me, Jamie. Tell *me.*"

"I can't. That's not the kind of person I am."

"I know," he whispered in her ear. "I know. Because we're alike, you and I. But for this moment, here, trust me. You can say anything. You can open your heart—"

"And then what?" she cried, jumping up. She stood in front of him, hugging her elbows, anger flashing in her eyes. "I can't do this, Edward. I don't want to. It frightens me."

"I know." He sighed, pressing his hands on his knees. He let his head drop between his shoulders, defeated. Then he looked up. A shadow of a smile, self-mocking, rueful, curved his mouth. "So . . . I'll finish my coffee and go."

"I'm sorry," she said.

"No, I'm the one who's sorry." He sat awhile longer, staring down at his hands. Then he lifted his face and his eyes met hers, the eyes of a powerful, confident, but tortured man.

Across the room Jamie could feel his power, his strength. And it was more than a physical thing; it was a strength of heart and soul. He possessed a courage she could barely fathom, a bravery she could admire but not hope to achieve. Oh, life was not going to defeat this man. Not him. Never.

The little child deep inside her reached out, seeking this strength and protection. And the woman she was reached out in an impulsive, rash, uncharacteristic rush of emotion. "Wait! Let me make a fresh pot of coffee, and we'll talk. *I'll* talk," Jamie added, blushing. "Don't leave yet. Let's just spend a little time together and see what happens. Okay?"

"Okay." He grinned, his dark eyes flashing. "Yes. Anything you say." He laughed, a soft, husky sound deep in his throat. "Talk about taking me by surprise! Jamie, tell me what I finally did right."

"Nothing." She laughed back, trying to reveal as little as possible of what she was feeling. "Don't you get cocky on me now. I still have my doubts about you."

She handed him a fresh cup, and their hands touched. Suddenly all her senses were on fire. She could smell the subtle spice of his cologne, see the golden highlights that ringed the black pupils in his eyes, feel the heat of his body across the little space between them. Quickly she tucked her hand into her pocket.

"Don't do that," he admonished, sliding his fingers down past her wrist and entwining them with hers. "Here . . . hold my hand. Let me touch you. Let yourself touch me."

She giggled like a schoolgirl, like a kid on a first date. But she held his hand. She sat down beside him on the couch, their thighs touching, their fingers laced. Warmth traveled up her arm, a sweet, lulling heat that melted her uncertainty. It was lovely. It was a delicious, soothing pleasure. She tipped her head sideways, leaning against his shoulder and looking up at his face. "This is nice," she whispered.

"I'm glad you think so too."

"And you're nice. A nice person. You'd be a good friend to have."

"Which is what I want to be," he answered, smiling down at her. He kissed her brow. "A good friend." Another kiss. "A best friend." And another. "A lover—"

She jerked back, but he caught her, held her gently but firmly by the arms, and kissed her again. This time he kissed her on the mouth, his lips warm and smooth, sweet as honey. "Those are good things to want, Jamie. Those are good things to be. Don't be frightened. Not of me. You don't have to be afraid of me."

He kissed her again, lightly, beseechingly, and her resistance fled, banished to the far recesses of her mind. Lifting his head to search her eyes, he read there what he was hoping for. He was smiling as he bent to kiss her again.

Eagerly Jamie leaned up against him, pressing her lips to his. Her hands found his face and lingered there, her fingertips grazing his cheeks, his temples. She pushed her hands through his hair, held his head in the curve of her small hands like a treasure she had just discovered. Oh . . . a sweet heat was rushing through her chest, her belly, down to the very core of her being. She felt golden and shining, melting and impetuous. Gathering her knees under her, she pressed her body hungrily against his.

With a groan Edward pulled her close, kissing her and whispering her name. Then he slid himself under her and pulled her down along the whole length of his body.

Jamie was shaking, laughing; she couldn't stop. She buried her face against his neck. "Mr. Rockford . . . I thought we were going to talk."

"Talk, my darling. I'm a captive audience."

She kissed his neck. "But how will I know you're listening?"

"I'm listening."

"But how will I know you're responding?"

"Trust me, Jamie," he growled. "I'm responding."

She bit his earlobe, a sharp little nip with her front teeth.

"Ow! What was that for?"

"For getting fresh with me."

"Fresh? Hell, I am an absolute paragon of restraint. Here I am. And here you are. And we both have our clothes on. If that's not restraint—" He laughed. Then he turned his face to her, one dark brow climbing in hopeful inquiry. "But I am open to other suggestions, my dear Ms. Payton."

She gave him a quick, wet kiss on the mouth, then pushed herself up and away. She tucked the unruly edge of her T-shirt back into her jeans, brushed the hair back out of her eyes. "I think we'd better stick to talk for a while, Mr. Rockford."

His groan was deep and heartfelt. But one look at her face and he swung his legs off the couch, planted his feet firmly on the floor. "Whatever you say, Jamie."

"Okay?"

"Of course okay." And then he smiled at her, a real smile, a beautiful smile filled with caring and honesty. A genuine smile . . . friend to friend, man to woman.

It made her eyelids sting with tears. Biting her lip, she reached out and brushed the thick, dark hair back from his eyes. "You do tend to surprise me, Edward. Surprise and amaze me." She swallowed hard, then forced a smile. A shrug came with it. "Can I get you anything? Do you want something to eat?"

"I'm fine. But I got you out of bed. You must be hungry."

"You know?" she replied, her eyes growing wide. "I *am* hungry. I haven't felt like eating for days, but suddenly I'm ravenous. I'll make eggs. How do you like your eggs?"

"None for me, thanks. But you go ahead. I'll—"

"No, I couldn't eat with you watching. Please have something. I can make pancakes. Or English muffins—"

"Muffins are great."

"Great! Okay. You sit there and I'll get everything ready."

"Do you mind if I look around?" Edward asked, standing and stretching, his arms locked behind his head, his hair all tousled.

His handsomeness made her tremble. She had to turn away to hide the arousal she was feeling. "Go right ahead," she said over her shoulder, and busied herself in the little kitchen space. "Truth is, there's not much to see. The canvases on the floor are all dry; you can look to your heart's content. Most of it's awful. The only thing you'd have to be careful of is the canvas on the easel. I was working on it late last night. It's the craziest thing—"

"Oh, my God."

Jamie spun.

Edward was standing in front of the easel, frozen in shock and disbelief. The look on his face made her skin crawl.

"What is it?" she whispered. "What's the matter?"

But he simply stared at the painting, one hand clutched to his head.

She hurried to his side. Gently, she touched his arm. "Edward?"

He turned to her slowly, his dark eyes wide, all pupils, black as coals. "That's my house."

Jamie thought she was going to faint. The room spun. Only he and the painting, those two fragments of reality, held firm. She dug her nails into his arm. "What did you say?"

He shook his head, speechless now, eyes narrowed, his dark brows lowered in fierce concentration.

"Edward, what do you see there? Tell me.

It's important!" Her voice was rising, along with a growing feeling of hysteria.

He stepped between her and the easel. "Jamie. How did you paint this? How? Who told you? Who showed you?"

She pressed her hands together, clutching them under her chin. "I don't know what you mean," she whispered. "Stop it. You're scaring me."

"*I'm* scaring *you*?" A sharp burst of laughter escaped from his throat. "How the hell do you think I feel? Here . . . in your painting . . . is my house! My *home*. The place I go to to escape, to hide, to leave the world behind. No one knows about it, no one. So who took you there? How did you know?" The last came out a whisper. Dragging his hand through his hair, he stared at her, shaken, reduced to silence.

Jamie lifted her chin. "Then . . . what you see there is a landscape, right? That's what you're telling me?"

He turned to stare at the painting. "Well, of course. I mean, what else is there to see? What do you mean?"

It was her turn to laugh, and hers was equally shaky and uncontrollable. "The thing is, Edward . . . nobody else sees it." She waved away his dismissal. "No, it's the truth.

They only see an abstract. My usual . . . well, perhaps better than usual . . . abstract. Shape and color. That's what it is supposed to be, and that's what they see. They *don't* see a landscape. *They don't see a house.*"

Talking had calmed her, or at least put a facade of normalcy over the whole odd situation. With a little shrug she slipped under his arm and stared at the painting. "It's strange, but I don't see it while I'm painting. Only later. But there are the hills, though I don't know what hills they are."

"The Shenandoahs," came his muffled reply. He had one hand over his mouth, his eyes half-closed.

". . . and the road. See?"

"Yes. Of course."

". . . here, the house."

"My house."

". . . a house. And a door. And here, the window . . ." She bent closer, peering at the painting now, scrutinizing the details. Her face was but inches away and she reached out as if to touch one small spot. Then her hand froze. In a very little voice she whispered, "I was painting very late last night and my eyes were so tired, and I didn't . . . well, as I said I never seem to know what I'm painting in this picture, but here, in the window. See? Someone is here in the window. And I can see who it is now. Look."

But when she turned toward him, Edward backed away. His hands were clenched at his sides, his shoulders were squared, but his eyes had a wild, dark look.

"No," he said. "No. Don't say anything else. Don't." He backed to the far end of the room and then leaned against the wall, breathing through parted lips.

She followed him and, without touching him, leaned against the wall next to him.

He didn't look at her. He just began to talk. "Tell me the truth. Someone gave you a picture of my house, right?"

She shook her head.

"Someone who saw us together that first night? Someone from the network? As a joke?"

She shook her head.

"Jamie . . . !"

"I told you, Edward, I wasn't even trying to paint a house. I was painting an abstract and this just happened."

"*Happened?* Earthquakes happen. Tidal waves happen. Paintings don't happen." He shook his dark head and drew a deep breath. "I give up, Jamie. If I believe you, then I don't have any idea what's going on. I don't even know what to say."

"Are we both crazy?" She laughed, shivering at the same time.

"I've been called many things, not all of them complimentary, but never crazy." Again he rubbed his eyes as if a headache were gathering there. "I don't know. I just don't know."

In the silence, Jamie stole a quick look at him. "Edward," she said softly, "would you take me there?"

That brought his eyes full to her face. He shook his head without thinking, an instinctive, long-practiced refusal.

"Why not?"

"I can't. I simply can't. I don't take anyone there."

She lifted both sandy brows questioningly. "Am I just anyone, then?"

"That's not what I said—"

"Then what *are* you saying?"

"Jamie, I . . . I'm not even going there. I might not be going there for months. It's far away. I use it very little, only when things get unbearable. When I need a place to escape, to hide—"

"You already said that."

"Then don't ask me again!"

"But I have to. And don't be angry with

me. You're the one who's been pushing this whole thing—"

"Me? Pushing? I told you, I've tried like hell to stay away. If I could have nailed my feet to the floor, I would have. It isn't my fault."

"Well, it certainly isn't mine! I didn't want to see you. I didn't want to even let you in this morning, remember? And I certainly didn't want to paint this painting . . . this terrible painting. You know, I should just destroy it!" And in two steps she was at the kitchen table, fumbling with the can of turpentine and a handful of rags.

And she would have done it, too, except that in a second he was behind her, his arms around her, his strong hands on hers, guiding the can back to the tabletop. "No. No, don't Jamie. Shhh . . . hey, it's going to be all right. Shh . . . don't do that."

"But it frightens me," she whispered.

"I know. It frightens me a little too. I don't understand it. It makes no sense in my normal world." He turned her within the circle of his arms and held her close against him, chest to knees. He smiled down at her, trying to mask the confusion in his dark eyes. "But my world has not been normal since the moment I met you. I suppose I should get used to surprises."

"And maybe it isn't a bad surprise," she whispered hopefully, her lips almost touching his throat. The steady beat of his pulse steadied her. She looked up. "Maybe it's some wonderful magic—"

He laughed, hugging her so tightly he lifted her off her feet. "I wouldn't say that to anyone else or people *will* think you're crazy."

"I don't care. All my life I've cared, but suddenly I don't anymore."

He laughed again, shaking his head. "Good. Fine. A sudden breakthrough, an epiphany! Just what we need now!"

She laughed with him, kissing the place where the pulse beat in his throat. "You said you'd get used to surprises—"

"Yes, I did." And hugging her, he looked over her head at the easel standing in the bright midday light. "Jamie?" he asked softly. "Who did you see in the window?"

She tipped her head back and gathered a big breath, as if she were about to perform some daring feat. "Me," she answered. "And I'm smiling."

Edward shut his eyes. The rhythm of his pulse changed, galloping suddenly. He swallowed. "Then I had better take you there. Can you be ready this evening? I have an afternoon meeting I can't postpone with the network president and the head of French programming, but I could be back by five. Six the latest. Can you be ready?"

"Yes. But are you sure?"

For the briefest instant doubt flickered behind his dark eyes. But he bent his head and kissed her on the lips. "I'll be back this evening. Be ready."

EIGHT

"May I turn on the radio?" Jamie asked after fifteen minutes of nerve-racking silence in the car.

"Sure. There are CDs in the compartment there. You're welcome to play whatever you like." Then Edward lapsed back into a stony silence.

This is a mistake, Jamie thought, staring down at the plastic boxes. She couldn't focus on the titles; all her concentration was focused on the man at her side. He was angry. He was sorry he'd ever agreed to take her along. It was evident in the thrust of his chin, the glowering darkness on his handsome face.

And to tell the truth, she didn't really want to be here. It had seemed fated, almost predestined from the safe vantage point of her loft, but now it felt foolish. What did she hope to prove? What did she think this was going to accomplish?

Edward heard the music begin, but it was muffled by the roar of sound in his head. His blood was pounding in his temples. Voices bludgeoned his brain: There's a meeting. . . . I need five minutes. . . . There's a problem only you can solve. . . . How did you want this worded? . . . You've got to be there! . . . Edward . . . Edward . . . Edward. And then his own harsh, condemning voice: What the hell do you think you're doing taking her there? You'll pay for this, Rockford . . . count the cost.

Damn!

They exchanged wary glances followed by tight, formal smiles as the little car zipped onto the freeway and left the city behind.

It was dusk. They drove with the lights on, and bits and pieces of the surrounding countryside flashed into existence and then disappeared. Jamie rolled her window halfway down to let in the evening air, hoping it would cool her flushed skin. The need to say something kept her tense and restless but her pride kept her silent. It was his car: let him talk!

Edward was afraid to open his mouth, afraid of what he'd say. Never before had he felt so out of control. Annoyance ran through him like a rat in a cage, its little claws digging at his insides. But it was his own damn fault, his and no one else's, certainly not this woman's.

He glanced across the dark interior and caught his breath. No wonder he no longer knew what he was doing! Look at her, the wind tugging at her hair, blowing it back from her small oval face, etching her lovely profile against the dark background of the passing landscape.

Landscape! *That* was the key to the whole problem. Damn! If it weren't for that painting, they wouldn't be here now. They wouldn't be heading for his hideaway in the hills. None of this would be happening!

If it weren't for the painting . . .

Edward felt as if someone had drawn their nails up his spine. The hair on his arms rose; his breathing quickened.

Suddenly the silence was more than he could stand. He said the first thing that popped into his head. "You know, the way you're sitting there, staring out the window, reminds me of my father. He loved to drive." Edward gave a low chuckle. "No, actually, he loved to *be* driven. He taught me to drive when I was twelve. And to fly when I was sixteen."

Jamie recognized an olive branch when it was offered. She gave a small sigh of relief and tucked her hair behind one ear. "Really? Is that legal?" she asked.

"We lived in northern Minnesota, he and I. There weren't that many people around to say legal or not. And anyway, my father was kind of a maverick."

"What did he do?"

"Flew fire-fighting planes for some independent outfit up there. The National Forest Service would call them in when a blaze got out of hand."

"That sounds terribly dangerous."

"He was so sure of himself, I never thought about the danger. If he did, he never let on."

"Is he still alive?"

"No. When he wasn't fire-fighting, he hired out for crop dusting. He died of emphysema about nine years ago."

"Oh, I'm sorry."

"Yes. Me too. We had good times together. We'd head out early in the morning, me driving, and he'd just stare out the window, soaking it all in like a sponge—the forests, the lakes, the little towns; he could name every one, tell whether the trees were healthy, whether there'd be fish in the lake. I used to joke with him, ask what the people were eating for dinner." He laughed again, then glanced at Jamie. "How about you? Were you close with your dad when you were growing up?"

Jamie felt a chill settle over her skin. She ducked back in her seat. "Not especially."

Edward looked at her. But instead of quickly changing the subject or filling in the awkward silence, he waited patiently. When she said nothing, he asked, "Why not?"

Jamie shrugged. "I was a grave disappointment to him, I guess." She felt again the old welling up of emotion, the sting behind her eyelids, the cold flame of anger. She wanted to say, "It's none of your business. Leave me alone!" But strangely, this time when she started to speak, it all turned upside down.

Grief engulfed her.

Rough-edged, her voice sounded hollow and ghostly. "We used to go on long drives too. We lived in Manhattan, but we had a weekend place up in Connecticut. We'd leave Friday evening when he'd get home from work, and he would make me ride up front with him. My mother liked to have the whole backseat; she'd take her satin pillow and sleep so she'd be rested for the parties later. So I'd sit next to him. And he'd quiz me about my week at school. With whom was I friends? To what committees had I been elected? For which class office was I going to run? And all the time outside the car window there were these hills, growing darker and more mysterious, the trees almost black, and so tall, so thick. I knew there were bears in there. Wolves! And deer, all dappled and light-footed. I wanted to be there with them. I wished I could jump out of the car and run through those woods. . . . But if he even caught me looking he'd say, 'Pay attention!' or 'What are you doing? Pouting again?' He hated pouting. He hated any emotion that showed weakness."

"The bastard! I'd like to rip his head off and stuff it down his throat."

Jamie gasped. Then she started to laugh. She buried her face in her hands, and her shoulders shook. When she looked up, she had to wipe her face with the back of her hand.

Edward put his hand on her knee and squeezed. "Are you laughing or crying, Jamie?"

"I don't know," she whispered. "I really

don't. After all these years I've never had the nerve to *think* that, let alone say it out loud."

"It's the truth."

"Maybe. But you just don't say that kind of thing to—or about—Mr. James C. Payton, Junior."

Edward threw her a startled glance. "J. C. Payton, Junior? InterCon Inc.? That's your father?"

Jamie nodded.

"But from something you said, the way you referred to him, I thought . . . I assumed your father was dead."

"That's how it feels to me. All I seem to have is the ghost of his voice in my head. A very nasty ghost."

He touched her cheek. "It's time to be done with ghosts, time for both of us, I think."

Jamie looked out into the darkness. But it was a small car, a small space, and he could easily hear her answer. "You're braver than I am, Edward. Stronger. Me, I've learned to live with it."

"But you shouldn't—"

"Shouldn't? Great. Just what I need is *another* man telling me what I should or should not be doing, should or should not be feeling!"

"Oops," he whispered, ducking his head repentantly. "Guess I did it again. Sorry."

"Forget it."

"No. I am truly sorry, Jamie. I didn't mean it to come out that way, dictatorial and chauvinistic, sounding like your father."

"But it did." Her mouth was set, but her chin was quivering.

"I'm sorry. All I wanted to say was that you're brave and strong also, and—"

"Me? You must have me confused with someone else."

"No, I don't. You are brave, passionate, courageous. No, don't argue with me. It's the truth. Case in point—you paint, don't you?"

He gave her just enough time to whisper yes before he plunged on. "And did your father want you to paint?"

"Are you kidding? He forbade it. He called it nonsense, trash, a waste of time. He laughed at me."

"So your mother came to your defense."

"My mother was happiest when she forgot I existed."

"But you paint." He looked at her, a slow grin spreading across his face. "You paint, don't you, Jamie Payton?"

Jamie pursed her lips, but couldn't keep an

answering grin from playing at the corner of her mouth. "Yes, I do. Edward Rockford."

"There. I rest my case. And my suggestion to you is, the next time he gives you any grief, tell him to stuff it."

"Sure."

"Try it. It might feel good."

"Oh, Edward, you make it sound so simple. It isn't."

"Of course it isn't, my sweet darling. If it were simple, it wouldn't have gone on and on, hurting you for all these years."

His gentleness disarmed her. Tears welled in her eyes. "I manage. Most of the time I can hold it at bay, the bad feelings, the sadness, but every so often it just fills my head, my heart. It's . . . it's hard to always be in control."

"I know, Jamie," he said, "I know. But I also know you deserve better. You deserve to be loved and praised and admired . . . not hounded by feelings from the past. Tell me about them, about the bad feelings."

She had been leaning toward him, drawn to the warmth of his words, but suddenly she pulled back. She shook her head.

He had to glance at her to realize how angry she was, how grim-faced and unmoving. "Jamie?"

She didn't answer, didn't even acknowledge him.

One dark brow rose. He could be stubborn too. "Jamie? What made you so angry?"

"I'm not angry."

He gave a sharp laugh. "Right! And the ocean's not salty. Oh, you're angry, all right—"

"I don't like to be pushed. I don't like my space invaded."

"Even by me?"

"And who are you?"

"The man who loves you."

The silence was complete. Absolute. The words stunned them both and they sat now, side by side, trying to figure out what in heaven's name to do next.

Edward shrugged and raked one hand through his hair. "I guess that caught us both by surprise."

Jamie nodded. Her eyes were wide as saucers and she turned them to him cautiously, checking out the set of his chin, the line of his mouth, the swoop of his brows. "I . . . I don't know what to say."

The sound he made was half groan, half laughter. "Well, that in itself says plenty."

"No, it's only that I . . . I didn't expect you to say that."

"And I didn't know I was going to. It just happened. Like your painting, Jamie." Again that mocking half laugh, a rough sound deep in his chest. Then he stiffened. "But I did think it was obvious."

"Oh."

"Yes. Oh." Then he added, "Otherwise I wouldn't be taking you here. I told you what this place means to me. I've never taken anyone here . . . until tonight."

Jamie began to tremble. She was breathing too fast, too shallowly. She knew the feeling, recognized the absurd onset of panic, but she never had been able to control it. Determined that Edward not see, she bent an elbow behind her head, leaned back, and closed her eyes.

His voice was warm as a touch, his touch so tender it brought unwanted tears to her eyes. "Go ahead, Jamie, get some sleep. I'll wake you when we're there."

And like the coward she believed she was, Jamie squeezed her eyes tight and prayed for sleep.

As Edward looked at the house waiting among the pines, doubt assailed him. What am I doing? he thought. Am I crazy? This is my sanctuary, the one safe place for me in this world. How can I be doing this? For an instant he toyed with the thought of turning around and bringing an end to all this foolishness. But that crazy painting *and* this beautiful woman were too compelling, moving him toward a destiny he no longer controlled.

He shook his head ever so slightly and muttered, "You're just going to have to see how this all plays out, Rockford. You don't have any choice."

Reaching over, he gently shook Jamie's shoulder. "Jamie . . . wake up. We're here."

"Wha-what?" she stuttered, still enveloped in the warm cocoon of sleep. "What's the matter?"

"Nothing is wrong, my sleeping beauty. We're here. Come, let me help you." Before she could protest, he had lifted her in his arms and was carrying her up the path toward the house.

She lifted her head, opening her eyes to the moonlight. And it was as if she had gone to sleep in the real world but awakened in a fairy tale. Edward was carrying her past the bramble hedge and there was the enchanted castle.

It was magic.

Because she knew this house, knew it with

her heart, her soul. What her eyes saw, her inner being named and claimed. This house, this wonderful house! She had glimpsed it in dreams. She had painted it with the magic paints. She saw immediately how the building was set on ancient stonework and the old stones held and cradled the house. She saw the stout stone chimney and could envision the cozy fire in the fireplace; she felt its warmth like a welcoming hug.

But habit made her pull back. She stiffened in his arms. Maybe they were going too fast. Maybe she was expecting too much.

"Jamie? What is it?" he asked, feeling how tense she'd suddenly become.

"It's nothing," she whispered against his chest. "I'm fine. You can put me down."

Her nervousness summoned up his courage. "Maybe I don't want to put you down," he teased, rubbing his cheek against hers. "Maybe I'll just carry you up to this meadow I know and keep you there all night, with clover for your blanket and stars for your roof."

"*Maybe* you're as scared as I am about going into the house." She gave him a knowing look, sandy brows lifted over wide gray eyes.

He set her down. A wry smile played across his lips. "Then there's only one thing to do, isn't there? Let's go." Taking her hand, he led the way up the wooden steps and across the wide front porch. He stopped at the door and took out a key.

Jamie swept her eyes over the facade. "Oh, Edward, it's really beautiful, even more so than I remembered."

"Remembered?" he echoed, hairs lifting on the back of his neck.

"Imagined!" she corrected quickly. "Dreamed. I don't even know anymore. But it is beautiful." She turned and touched the flat of her palm to the front door. The wood was polished smooth as silk; beneath her hand it felt as warm and alive. She touched the knocker, hand-carved in the shape of a wren. She lifted it, let it drop, and listened for the echo of sound she knew she'd hear reverberating through the rooms she could already envision.

"You can go in, Jamie," Edward whispered, pushing the door open.

But as she always seemed to do, Jamie surprised him. She held out her hand. "Walk in with me, Edward. We have to walk in together."

His chest rose and fell, giving no sign of the pain that shot like an arrow through his heart. Everything, each word, each gesture, the very stars above, seemed to hold some strange and wonderful significance. He drew a deep breath and clasped her hand in his.

He had walked through this door a hundred times. But never like this.

Thc fire was snapping on the hearth, set by the caretaker as he had asked it to be. But tonight it seemed a fairy fire, dancing and crackling like spirits in a ring.

The ceiling soared above, crossed by wooden beams hewn from trees on the surrounding land. Tonight the forest seemed to have moved indoors with all its dark mystery.

It was his house, and yet not his. It was his home. It was her painting.

They stepped inside together and the strangest, most subtle motion seemed to stir in the air around them. Beneath their feet, so faint and far below, the earth seemed to shift. It was all the same, and it was all different.

"Do you like it?" Edward whispered.

"I love it!" She laughed, the sound so free and spontaneous you'd think she'd left all her cares on the porch. "It's perfect, Edward. Perfect! And so much of it is you! I can't believe I never saw that before: how much the house *is* like you." Playfully, she pursed her lips, stiffened her chin, squared her shoulders, miming the words as she spoke them. "Look at it—big and bold. All these sure, stern lines and untouched planes. Unembellished. A tiny bit severe. But handsome. Magnificent. *And* with its few cozy spots . . ." She looped an arm through his and leaned against his shoulder, grinning up at him.

It made his heart stop. This was what he had wished for, what he had always longed for. But—

Oblivious to his turmoil, Jamie hugged him and danced away. "Look at this fire! I knew there'd be a fire. And I love this couch. Let's see, there's four . . . no, five pillows. I knew there were pillows. And this window. See?" She walked to the window, and without a wisp of hesitation, she pushed the curtain back and stood framed against the darkness, staring out. "See? It's me. In the window. See?"

Again the earth shook, a private tremor echoing in his soul. Edward envied her her sudden sureness, her want of caution, her unexpected certainty. In his heart he felt a splinter of fear and confusion. What was going on here? What was happening to the two of them? The realist in him demanded answers. There had to be answers.

"Come here," Jamie whispered from across the room. But before he could respond, she had begun moving slowly, languidly toward the hearth. "Come here, Edward. Come over here near the fire."

He licked at dry lips. His heart pounded. This was not the answer he had meant, but it was irrefutable.

Jamie smiled at him. "Come here, Edward. Come look at the fire with me. Look how it dances with joy. Look how the flames spark, orange and blue, their hearts on fire. Look how they writhe and leap. Come here . . . don't be afraid."

"Oh, I am not afraid." His voice was a husky growl. "But perhaps I'd better stay over here."

"No, come here. I have something to tell you."

His blood was racing. His breath was coming quick and harsh and he had to lick his dry lips again. But it was like hearing a siren's song. He was powerless suddenly, his resistance weakening. "You can tell me while I'm over here."

"But I can't show you. Come over here and let me show you."

Staring at her from beneath half-lowered lids, Edward began to smile, his lips curving down at the corners.

Jamie saw all the sensuality latent in that loose, hot smile. It ignited an impatient excitement in her. She was desperate to touch him, to kiss him. "Come here to me," she whispered one last time, knowing she wouldn't have to say it again.

When he moved to within inches of her, when he bent his head and kissed her mouth, when he took her in his arms, all Jamie had to do was answer as she hadn't known she could until this very moment. Now. Here. It was destined to be this way.

Wrapping her arms around his neck, she kissed him back, lips parted, savoring the taste of him, his heat and passion. With her face pressed to his cheek she breathed in the warm, slightly spicy scent of his skin. He was delicious, mouthwatering. She pressed her lips to his neck and felt a shudder run through him. The groan that tore from his throat undid her. A surge of impetuous longing swept over her, chasing away thought. She tightened her arms around his neck and nibbled her way across his jaw back to his sweet, waiting mouth.

Edward's response was wild and fervent. Still holding her, whispering her name over and over against her lips, he sank to his knees, then down onto the hearth rug. Warmed by the fire, the wool was thick and soft as fur.

Without a thought, Jamie leaned back and drew him down on top of her, wrapping her legs around the lean, hard length of him. Propriety be damned. The only thing that mattered was the feel of the man holding her, the shape and form and being of this one particular man . . . this man she loved. There! It was said! No more hiding, no more pretending. A huge weight seemed to lift from her heart.

All of a sudden she was aflame with desire and free of inhibition. She pushed her fingers through Edward's thick dark hair and pressed her mouth against his. Her tongue slipped across his lips, stroking the sweetness that lay there, and then, when he groaned again as she knew he would, she slid her tongue inside his mouth. Daring! Crazy! Wonderful!

She'd never done anything like this, *never.* Only dreamed. Only wished. And here she was, initiating this . . . this what? This seduction! The thought made goose bumps rise along her skin. Oh, she loved it! Excitement made her dizzy, that and the fact that Edward was doing things she had only dreamed about. His mouth was everywhere, his tongue rasping across her skin, his hands trailing fire, his broad chest pinning her to the ground, a willing captive, but captive still.

Suddenly he stopped. He found her mouth again for another deep, stirring kiss, then straight-armed his weight off her so that he leaned over her, looking deep into her eyes.

Jamie was afraid he was going to say something, ask for reasons, expect some sane answer. "Oh, Edward!" she breathed, on the edge of tears, trembling.

But he knew now all that he needed to know. He flashed a wide, exultant grin, his body hard with desire, his sensuality blatant and fierce. Then he rolled off her and began to unbutton his shirt.

It made Jamie grin right back. She felt wild, careless, free. "Wait," she whispered, "Let me."

She unbuttoned his shirt, slowly, then pulled the tails slowly from inside his slacks. She spread the shirt open across his chest, exposing dark hair above a pristine white T-shirt. She kissed both, starting on the white cotton, and drawing her mouth slowly up the V and the bare skin of his throat. She felt his pulse there, hammering beneath her lips. His skin was warm. Soon he'd be sweating, and the dark hair would tighten, curl against that bronze skin. His nipples would harden. His chest would heave, his labored breathing straining against the cage of his ribs, his breastbone. His heart would pound.

She knew this. Knew it as though she

could feel it already, just as she knew how her body would be wet and aching, pulsing, yearning. She knew it already, though nothing had happened yet . . . and yet everything would. Soon. Soon! The anticipation was almost as delicious as the reality. One heightened the other. Already her palms were wet, her breasts tingling. Already, deep within her, she'd begun to ache and throb.

Grinning like a Cheshire cat, all grin now, all anticipation and desire, Jamie pulled his shirt down over his shoulders, off his arms, and tossed it away. Then she grabbed hold of the bottom of his T-shirt and pulled it up, and almost off, but left him trapped inside the white cotton, he the captive now while she kissed his chest, there on his collarbone, there just over his heart, there . . . first one hard nipple, then the other, her teeth nipping lightly.

Edward groaned and yanked the shirt off, free again, unrestrained, dangerous now. Dangerous and ready. A laugh, deep and husky, almost a growl, rose in his throat. Without a word, his dark eyes gleaming, he caught the bottom of her shirt in his hands and drew it off in one swift motion like a magician's trick.

Then his dark hair was brushing against her ribs. His mouth followed, tracing wet patterns across her skin. His mouth found her breasts and he kissed her lightly through the soft fabric of her bra. Then harder. Her nipples hardened, tingling, aching, and his mouth urged them on, hot and wet, the silky bra wet and clinging until he reached behind her back, the first touch of his hands on her bare skin, and undid the bra. It fell to the floor. Her shorts followed and then her panties.

Jamie trembled, head to toe. For an instant, from habit, she felt vulnerable, exposed, frightened, imperfect: not good enough, not pretty enough, not—

"You are so beautiful, so beautiful. . . ." Edward whispered, his voice clothing her in beauty, in praise.

And suddenly she was golden, a goddess!

Never, ever before . . . but now! Yes! "Yes," she whispered back, smiling even as the tears slid from the corners of her eyes. "And you are beautiful too! So beautiful, so wonderful, so amazing—"

He laughed, the sound husky now, lusty and sexy. "You haven't seen anything yet."

"You're right!" She laughed back, and reached up and unbuttoned his pants. She pulled them down, tugging them over his hips, sliding them down his thighs. But she could not . . . dared not . . . do the same to his boxers. Oh, they were great boxers: dark burgundy silk with bright trout printed across them. She touched them lightly, with just her fingertips. A trout stirred, heading upstream! She grinned, eyes narrowed, biting her lower lip. Ohmygosh, *I* made that happen! Power surged through her like a jolt of electricity. Even her fingertips sizzled!

"Go on," he groaned.

She shook her head, laughing. "I can't!"

"Oh yes, you can!" He laughed, leaning back on his elbows, his head dropping back between his shoulders, eyes closed. She could see the pulse beating in his throat. His skin was wet with sweat. "Go ahead," he breathed.

He was so beautiful! All bronze and gold in the lamplight, broad planes of hard muscle, umber shadows of dark hair, clean sharp angle of jaw, collarbone, hip; curve of muscle along his shoulders, ripple of muscle across his belly, thrust of muscle there, still hidden, but responsive to the slightest touch . . .

A gasp, his breath hissing between clenched teeth. "Oh God, Jamie . . . you're killing me. Go on. . . ."

So she did.

And then he was as naked as she, as vulnerable . . . and as eager, as daring. They touched and kissed, rolling like puppies on the rug, learning the feel, the taste, the strength and fragility of each other's bodies, learning each other's secrets, each other's pleasures.

"Yes . . . yes, there . . ." she whispered, curving her body to his touch.

"Oh yes, oh . . . oh, Jamie," he groaned, curving over her, fitting his body to hers. "Oh, Jamie! Oh, dear one! Sweet, sweet as honey, sweeter to my tongue, sweeter than—"

"Oh! Oh, Edward, yes! Oh, do that again! Oh, do something else—"

"What else? What do you want me to do, Jamie?"

"You know! Oh, Edward, please—"

"What? What do you want to do, Jamie. Tell me. Please. Tell me now—"

"I . . . I can't. But you know—"

"Tell me, love. Tell me—"

"Make love to me, Edward. Now. Now!"

Dropping back onto one elbow, he reached for his slacks and fumbled in one pocket.

Jamie heard the reassuring crinkle of foil and lifted up to kiss his chest. "My hero!" she whispered.

"Which is what I want to be," he whispered back, covering her completely with his warm, hard body.

"Which is what you are!" she said, opening herself to him, taking him in.

They made love then, on the rug, in the near dark, and when she came, she felt things she had never felt before, never even dreamed of! He climaxed with her, and his voice broke the stillness of the dark house. Giggling, Jamie pressed her face into the curve of his shoulder, rubbing her cheek against his skin. He laughed aloud, kissed her ear, and whispered something, the words muffled by his own shuddering laughter.

"Hmmm?" she murmured, already sliding away into a sweet delirium.

"I love you," he whispered again, and kissed her hair. And then, still holding her tight, he fell asleep also, a smile on his lips.

NINE

Jamie woke with sunlight on her face. A light blanket was spread over her from toes to shoulders. Underneath it she was bare as a newborn babe.

"Edward?" she whispered, propping herself up on one elbow. But she was alone on the couch, alone in the spacious, sunlit living room.

Edward! She crushed one fist to her mouth even as the memory swept over her like a storm. Had it truly happened? Had she dreamed it all? Was she dreaming even now?

Her eyes swept the room, seeking reality and finding instead images imbued with that strange and mysterious aura of fantasy: the house resting on its ancient stones, the huge hearth, the rug where she and Edward Rockford had lain and loved each other.

Oh! *That* was the image she could neither flee nor believe, the two of them making love, wildly, passionately, with total abandon. Her heart was bursting with the thrill of it . . . and the possibility that love had found her. What magic was making this happen . . . this painting, this house, this man?

Powered by happiness, she leaped up from the sofa, clutching the blanket to her chest. "Edward?" she called, her voice echoing through the empty house. Where was that man? She wanted him, wanted him *now.*

Bare feet slapping against the wooden floors, she roamed from room to room. She started in the kitchen, envisioning him seated at the far end of the table, drinking strong coffee from his favorite mug. The mug was there, but Edward was gone. She moved surely to his study, a cool shadowed room filled with books, then on through a small guest room. It was from there, at the bottom of that bed, that he had taken the blanket she wore now.

She hurried on to his bedroom with its king-size bed and solid oak furniture, a fireplace flanked by an overstuffed chair with an afghan thrown over the arm. It was a comfortable room, sunny yet cool in the morning light, the kind of room she'd want for herself: a room to be peaceful in, a room to be happy in. Of course, she'd want to set her easel there by the window; the afternoon light would filter in through the leaves of the trees outside, all soft and golden. And she'd like a dog. This was definitely a room for a dog, some big old hound whose tail would thump contentedly in the lovely quiet.

She saw it all as clearly as if she were painting the scene, brush in hand. And for once the picture in her head left her heart singing.

She quickly took a detour right into his bathroom with its huge claw-footed tub. She turned on the tap, splashed in shampoo to make bubbles, and climbed in. Oh, it was wonderful! She forgot her worries, leaned back, sank under, let her head roll back against the smooth, cool porcelain, and closed her eyes. She hadn't even shut the door! Let him come in, she thought. Let him find me! Come on, Edward Rockford! I'm waiting for you!

"Good morning."

"Yikes!" Jamie gasped, sinking nose-deep in bubbles. Her boldness vanished faster than water down a drain. "I . . . I didn't hear you!

I mean, I hope you don't mind my just making myself at home—"

Edward walked over and sat on the edge of the tub. "I don't mind at all. That's how I want you to feel." He brushed the wet hair back from her face, and though he touched her nowhere else, his dark gaze caressed her, seeming to pierce through bubbles, through water. He drank her in like a man dying of thirst.

His adoration was a heady brew! A smile gathered on Jamie's lips and spilled over into her eyes. Her daring was back. "So, where have you been all morning?"

Matching her grin, he stretched out one long, jean-clad leg and leaned over the tub to kiss her. "I was getting a surprise ready for you." He kissed her again, his tongue parting her lips and finding hers. "Mmmm, you kiss good!" he announced. "That's important."

"It is, huh? Well, I'm glad I passed the test!" She laughed.

"Me too! I intend to spend a lot of time kissing you, woman."

Jamie shivered, pleasure running over her skin like fingers. "You do, do you? Well, we might as well start now!" And without a thought she wrapped her arms around his neck and kissed him back, her tongue rasping across the smooth sweetness of his lips.

Edward groaned, the sound rising from deep in his chest.

Jamie thrilled to hear it. Such joy! Such power! It made her wild, made her crazy. She could do anything, absolutely anything right now, even pull this gorgeous hunk right into the bath with her!

"Don't even think about it!" Edward laughed again, bracing his hands on the edge of the tub. "If I get in there with you, we're not getting out! You've had it, woman!"

"You're not scaring me, Mr. Rockford!" she tossed back, all flashing eyes and bravado.

"Feeling feisty, aren't you?" He grinned. "Oh, you are a woman of constant surprises, Ms. Payton, and many temptations. But—" Reaching up, he loosened her wet arms from around his neck. "I have just spent the morning making extravagant plans for you and I'm not about to have them thwarted." He handed her a huge, fluffy towel. "Get out of that tub and meet me out front."

"Oh, Edward." She pouted, tilting her head and wrinkling her nose.

"Don't you try to cast a spell on me, you enchantress. Up and out of there!" And he strode through the door.

Jamie hugged herself. This couldn't be happening, could it? Had she lost her mind? *Was* she under some spell, some magic enchantment?

She no longer knew or cared.

In no time flat she was standing at the front door in jeans and a sweatshirt, her hair still wet and clinging to her head, one hand shading her eyes as she squinted out into the sunlight. But for some inexplicable reason, she was reluctant to step outside.

"Hello there," Edward called, appearing around the corner of the house.

Jamie's heart knocked against her ribs. "Hi!" She smiled but didn't move.

He grinned at her. "Do you want breakfast first or are you ready for some excitement?"

She pressed one hand to her chest, laughing. "I couldn't eat. I feel like I'm *living* on excitement! I've never felt this way."

"Then let's go!" he urged, expecting her to run down the porch stairs and into his arms. But she hesitated there in the doorway. "What?" he asked. "What is it?"

A shadow darkened Jamie's eyes. "I don't know," she whispered, and started to turn away.

"Jamie!" His tone stopped her and

brought her eyes back to his face. "Jamie, what is it? You can tell me anything."

Jamie shrugged. When she did speak, it was in a very little voice. "It sounds crazy, but I'm afraid to leave. To step outside. I'm so happy here. I just don't want it to disappear."

Edward raced up the steps and took her in his arms. "Oh, my darling, it won't disappear! It's real and solid as this house." Reaching out, he patted the old stones fondly. "Don't be afraid. Today, for us, the whole world is enchanted. Trust me." He bent and kissed her, then stood holding her in his arms.

When Jamie looked up, she could see her own amazing happiness mirrored in his dark eyes. His confidence filled her heart. "Yes, Edward, I do." She nodded, her eyes shining. "So . . . what are we waiting for?" Holding his hand, she danced down the steps.

At the bottom Edward took a sharp left, leading her toward a fenced pasture and a barn just beyond. "You'll need some decent boots," he said, talking as he walked. "There are extras in the barn. We're going riding."

"What?" Jamie yelped, putting the brakes on.

"Come on, you'll love it. I rounded the horses up early this morning and drove them down from the high pasture. Now they're saddled and ready. Lunch is packed. Everything is perfect."

"Oh, you've gone to so much trouble." She bit her lip. "I just don't know, Edward. Maybe I should stay here, sit on the porch and get some sun, breathe in this delicious country air. You could go for a ride without me—"

"I don't want to go without you. I don't want to do *anything* without you." He took her in his arms.

"Edward, really," she protested weakly. "I don't think I'll be very good at this—"

"You'll be wonderful."

Reluctantly she followed him across the yard. "I have to warn you, the only time I've ridden was back in summer camp. I was thirteen years old."

"Don't worry. It's like riding a bicycle."

"Oh no. I don't do *that* very well either."

He laughed and slipped an arm around her waist, pulling her close. The feel of him gave her a smidgen of confidence. "How big is my horse?" she managed to ask. "What's his name? How far are we going? Do you ride western or English?"

Laughing, Edward lifted her clear off her feet and swung her around. "So many questions! So many worries! Just relax, dear one. Have fun."

He put her down at the door to the barn. A dog was lying there, a big black Lab with his nose resting on his paws. His head looked as big as some whole dogs Jamie had seen. His ears pricked up at the sound of Edward's voice. "This is Dante," Edward said by way of introduction.

At the sound of his name, the dog rose and stood next to his master's leg, his eyes raised, all attention and adoration. "Good boy," Edward said, rubbing the big smooth head. "This is Jamie. A special friend. Be good to her."

As if he understood, Dante moved closer and placed his velvet muzzle in Jamie's hand.

She dropped to her knees, rubbing her cheek against his huge head. "What a beautiful dog," she said. "I love him."

"I think the feeling's mutual." Edward grinned and lifted the latch on the heavy wooden door. It was a small cozy barn filled with the sweet smell of hay and the warm animal smell of horses. One, black as coal, whickered as they entered. A chestnut lifted its head and looked at her with a dark, fierce eye.

Jamie stopped dead in her tracks, feeling suddenly small and fragile. The horse's hooves were huge! Its back was broad as a barrel. And it didn't like her; she was certain of that, just as she was certain that *this* beast was the horse she'd be riding. "Why are all your animals king-size? Couldn't you have a nice little Shetland pony stashed in here somewhere?"

Edward just laughed. "Here we go," he announced, striding back past her with the reins to both horses gathered firmly in his hands. "Follow me and I'll help you mount up."

Outside, sure enough, Edward was standing alongside the big chestnut, one hand on its head, the other on her stirrup.

"Got a stepladder?" she asked, making a face at him.

He laughed again, a rich, husky peal of laughter that rang in the morning air. "Come on. You'll love it."

"That's what you think!" From on top, the ground looked very far away to Jamie, distant and precious. When her horse shifted his weight, she grabbed his mane. "Good horse. Good boy. Whoa!"

Edward swung up into the saddle, then walked his horse over next to hers. Both his hands were resting lightly on the pommel. His long legs, in jeans and boots, seemed made for horseback. He looked dashing, elegant, a dark striking figure on a coal-black steed, like a knight of the Round Table, she fancied, a dark-haired Galahad, a bold Lancelot.

"Stirrups all right?"

Startled, she glanced down at her feet. "Fine, I think."

"Ready?"

"As ready as I'll ever be," she groaned.

"Then let's go. We'll take it slow at first—"

"At *first*?"

He laughed. "No more than a trot. Just follow me."

He turned his horse and headed across the open meadow. Dante was at his heels. The chestnut, without even waiting for her command, followed.

Oh, great, Jamie thought. Who is in control here? But she held tight and let her horse move slowly in the other's wake.

The grass was tall and wet with dew. Wildflowers bent and swayed in the breeze. The air smelled sweet and green. Under her, the horse rocked back and forth, side to side in a steady, comforting motion. Hey! This was easy. Now, what did she remember? Heels down. Knees tight. Hands even and easy on the reins. Back straight—

"Like it?" Edward called, half turning in his saddle to gaze at her.

"I love it!" she yelled back.

"Told you! You look like you were born to ride."

Her smile widened. "Thanks. I feel good. I think he likes me."

"He's crazy about you. You've won all our hearts!"

She didn't say anything, didn't have to. She was grinning from ear to ear. If she'd had a cowboy hat, she'd have waved it over her head. Twirled her lasso! Polished her spurs! Do-si-doed and sashayed with the best of 'em. Oh, he made her feel wonderful, absolutely wonderful!

It must have been obvious, because a moment later he turned his horse and pulled back beside her. He held the reins loosely in one hand, and with the other he brushed the hair back from her face. "You're glowing. Positively glowing! If I had known it had this effect, I would have taken you riding last night," he added with a mischievous wink.

Jamie blushed madly. It was the first mention either of them had made of the night before. Immediately, the whole scene was conjured up before her eyes: the two of them on the floor, the rug, the blazing fire, the light and shadows on his beautiful body, the touch, the sounds, the heat. . . .

Her cheeks flamed.

"What's this?" He laughed, narrowing his eyes to see her better. "Are you blushing? How could anyone so passionate, so sensual, so wild—"

"Edward!"

He threw back his head and roared.

Pressing her lips together, chin up, Jamie gave her horse a good kick and trotted beyond his reach—but not beyond the sound of his laughter. It was contagious and soon she was giggling, bumping along with her shoulders shaking. Oh, this man! This man! Why couldn't he just be average, ordinary, predictable, controllable? Why couldn't she keep her cool? Why couldn't—

"Jamie!" He had galloped up to her and now he was so close, his thigh was pressing against hers. "Jamie—" He'd lowered his voice so that she had to strain to hear him, had to lean out over the saddle toward him.

"What?"

He circled her neck with one arm, pulling her close, bending his dark head toward hers and kissing her fiercely, hungrily. "I love you."

His horse whinnied; hers did a nervous little sidestep.

"Oh!" she gasped.

"It's all right." Dropping his reins, he reached over and lifted her clear out of the saddle, held her on his lap for a moment and then set her on the ground. In one motion he swung his leg over the pommel and dropped down beside her.

"Oh," she breathed. "Oh, Edward . . ."

A blanket appeared, a blue square in the midst of all the wildflowers. Magic again, like the words he had just spoken. Oh, had he really said those words out here in the daylight, in the bright light of reality? Had he said them so passionately? Had he meant them truly? Why else did her heart pound so? Why else did her blood sing in her veins? Why else did her soul rejoice?

Taking both her hands in his, Edward sank onto the blanket and pulled Jamie down on top of him. He wrapped his long legs around her and held her close, whispering in her ear such soft words, such sweet words that tears stung behind her lids. Oh, they really shouldn't, Jamie thought. Oh . . . they should take things slowly; they should talk, ride, anything but this . . . this lovely touching, this sweet kissing, this melting together.

Thoughts vanished. Out of the corner of her eye she saw a horse's head appear, reins dangling, teeth munching happily on the sweet green grass, the picture of contentment.

And here was all this sweet green grass beneath her. And clear blue sky above her. And a man in her arms who loved her. Oh, a man whom *she* loved! She had to tell him, had to say it also. Don't be afraid, she told herself. Not any longer. Just tell him. . . .

But before she could, there was the crush of his mouth on hers, the touch of his hands, the delicious weight of his body. His heat, his strength, his desire, his tenderness, his teasing and adoration, all of it mixed together into a marvelous potion, a magic potion, an elixir that chased away thought and fear and left only the joy of their lovemaking.

Later she lay on her back, watching the slow dance of the clouds, holding his hand.

This time she would not fall asleep, even though her body was washed through with stillness, with peace and happiness. Her limbs were made of butter, melting in the sun. Arms, legs . . . they existed. She could feel them. But she couldn't move them on a bet! Her head was floating on clouds and resting on a pillow of daisies, all at the same time. Her breath—she could feel her chest rise and fall, could feel the sweat on her breasts drying in the cool touch of the breeze—but her breath was *his* breath also, nourishing both their hearts. It was real; it was true: love let them share even the same breath.

She turned her head and smiled at him.

Edward smiled back, his dark hair tousled again, falling over his forehead. His dark eyes were half-closed, his lips parted. He had that look again, that look that fevered her blood, the look of some romantic poet, some hero . . . someone from another time, another place. He was a man who was more than just a man, stronger, more heroic, more daring than anyone in real life ought to be.

Trembling, she rolled over onto her side and touched his face. So beautiful. So incredibly handsome! She touched his lips and he opened his mouth and kissed her fingertips. It thrilled her. A mere kiss should never be able to do this. But wait, I'll try it again, she thought, and again the feel of his mouth dizzied her. She leaned closer, placed her lips on his, and felt her heart soar. "Oh . . ." she whispered softly, the words out before she knew it. "Oh, I love you, Edward. I do."

"Then why are you shaking so, my darling?" he whispered back, gathering her in his arms.

"Because I've never been this happy. It's . . . it's like . . ." She stuttered to a stop, wide-eyed and speechless.

He held her at arms' length, his eyes questioning. "What? What were you going to say?"

"For what I'm feeling, Edward," she answered softly, drawing a fingertip across his lips. "I don't have any words, any experience. That's what I just realized. For me to say how I'm feeling, I'd have to invent a whole new vocabulary."

"Then we'll invent it together," he said softly, pulling her close against his warm flesh. "Now this"—he kissed her nose—"means 'I love you.' And this"—he kissed her lips—"means 'I adore you.' And this"—he slipped a hand up under her sweatshirt, his fingertips grazing her breasts—"this means—"

"I know exactly what that means!" She laughed. "And I'm all for it!"

Hours later, after wine and bread and cheese, they began the ride home. This time Jamie was in the lead. The chestnut, having gotten only an apple from their picnic lunch, was heading quickly for the barn. Jamie merely held the reins; she didn't even have to steer. She rode along in a sort of daze, the sun warm on her head, the flowers brushing against her boots until the leather was dusty with pollen, her head filled with dreams.

She stole a look at Edward. Oh, he was so unbelievably handsome, it took her breath away. That face. That body. That sensuality that clung to him like an aura. She'd never get enough of him. Never! Maybe when they reached the house, dusty as they were, they could try out that old claw-footed tub and see if it really *was* big enough for two!

Grinning, she stole another peek over her shoulder.

"What are you up to now, woman?" Edward laughed, spurring his horse up next to hers. "I caught that look!"

"It was lust. Pure lust," she admitted, laughing back at him happily.

His smile widened, a flash of white teeth, a leap of desire in his own dark eyes. Surprise! And delight! "I want at least a hundred years to do nothing but love you, Jamie Payton. I suspect it may take that long to get to know all of you."

"Me?" She was absolutely amazed by the thought. She gave a low chuckle, a little lift of her shoulders. "I'll take the hundred years, happily—but honestly, I'm not that complicated."

One dark brow rose. "I think you are. I

think you are like those roses, those pink roses I gave you—petal upon petal, layer upon layer, each as lovely as the first, changing and unfolding in constant beauty."

Jamie was speechless. Tears welled on her lower lids and spilled down her cheeks.

Edward paled. He curved a hand behind her head. "Jamie? What's the matter? What did I do?"

She caught his hand and pressed it to her lips. "Nobody . . . *nobody* has ever said anything that beautiful to me."

"Their mistake," he answered, the color returning to his face. "Hell, you scared me!"

"I'm sorry. You caught me by surprise." Her voice was still shaky, but her eyes were shining with happiness. "Oh, Edward, can this be real?"

He took her shoulders roughly in his hands and stared deep into her eyes. "Yes. It can be . . . it *is* real. I promise."

A strange mood settled over them both. Quiet, pensive, they let their horses walk slowly, heads down, grazing at the tall green grass. Neither was in a hurry to get back. All of nature seemed to enfold them in a sweet mystery the way the house had done last night. So, when they crossed a little stream,

Jamie impulsively pulled the chestnut to a stop and slid off.

"Can we sit here for a little while?" she asked.

"Whatever you'd like." Edward tied the two horses to some low willow branches, then threw a stick into the stream for Dante, who jumped into the game—and the water—with a big doggie grin.

"Oh, you're a great dog!" Jamie applauded when he carried the stick right back up the stream bank to Edward.

"Give it to *her*," Edward instructed, pointing at Jamie.

Dante obediently dropped the stick at Jamie's feet. She patted the wet shaggy head and tossed the stick even farther upstream. She had to laugh as Dante bounded and splashed from rock to rock, pawing at one submerged stick then another, determined to find just the right one. "I'm not fussy!" she called to him, laughing. "Bring me anything! Here, Dante!"

Edward was sitting farther up the grassy knoll, leaning against a rough old pine and watching them.

Jamie turned and tossed a pine cone at him, hitting him on the thigh. When he didn't play, she tossed another, hitting him squarely in the lap. That roused a sexy grin. "I thought you wanted to sit and enjoy the scenery, Jamie."

"I am."

"Uh-huh."

"I am! I just didn't want you to think I was ignoring you."

"That's all right. I'm quite content for the moment."

"You are, are you?" she teased. Standing, she brushed twigs and leaves off her bottom, then sauntered on up the slope. "Actually, you look a little lonely to me. Forlorn. In need of company."

Excitement smoldered in Edward's dark eyes. She could see him struggling for composure, and losing.

The awareness of his response excited her. That's the way it was between them, this constant circle of awareness and excitement, as if for the first time she was both truly alive and connected to another living, breathing being. Whole herself, and yet part of something more. One . . . and yet two. Again, a wave of dizzying happiness swept over her, leaving her shaken, opened.

"Here, come sit with me," Edward said, pulling her gently down onto his lap. "You've got that look again."

"What look?" She laughed breathlessly, letting her head fall against his shoulder.

"This one—" he whispered, touching her face with the backs of his fingers. "It wraps itself around my heart and squeezes. I . . ." He swallowed, shook his dark head. "I can't decide if what I'm feeling is pleasure . . . or pain."

"Oh, Edward, I want it to be pleasure. I wouldn't ever want to cause you pain." She pulled his head down so that their lips met and kissed him hungrily, greedily, feeling her whole body react to the feel of him, the taste of him. One kiss and she was melting, the petals opening. . . .

"Oh!" she gasped. "I really do believe there is some magic between us, Edward. Somehow you seem to know things about me that I don't even know, or that I've kept hidden for years. And here I am, *me* . . . the same me I've always been, and yet so different I hardly know myself. I don't even know what I'm going to say or do next. I don't know what to *expect*. My Lord, I think I've gone beyond expectations, to really *feeling* and *being*. *Me*, who planned every day from cornflakes to conversations. It's unbelievable! Ha!" She threw back her head, threw her arms wide, and laughed. "Heavens! No one would recognize me now!"

He laughed with her, holding her, his eyes saying everything.

Jamie wrapped her arms around his neck, speaking quietly now, almost solemnly. "You did it, Edward Rockford. It's all your doing."

"No, Jamie," he said softly, matching her tone. "You did it yourself. It's always been there in you, all of it, the happiness, the daring, the"—he allowed himself a grin, wiggling his eyebrows at her—"the wild free woman."

"But you woke her up. You called her by name! And I thank you. And I *don't* want any arguments," she added, kissing him again.

"The last thing I want to do is argue. I've done enough of that all my life."

"Not here. Not now. Not with me," she crooned, kissing his chin, his neck, the pulse beating in the hollow of his throat. She slipped her hands beneath his shirt and rubbed his chest. She could feel his muscles tighten, his quick intake of breath.

"I'll go get the blanket," he said.

"I'll be your blanket," she whispered, and without a thought she pulled her sweatshirt over her head, unbuttoned her jeans. The breeze and the warm sun caressed her bare skin. She felt wicked and free, free of inhibitions, free of fears, free to lie naked with her lover for all the world to see. And when Edward was naked also, she kissed his body, each golden plane and hollow, each curve of muscle and angle of bone. She touched his flesh, learning its beauty, memorizing it, exploring it with an artist's eye and a lover's touch.

She let time stop, or rather it seemed that she slipped out of time, into the timelessness of being, of touching, of feeling and loving. The sun shone. The grass was soft and sweet. She was here, now. And he was here, now. And that was all there was.

. . . and Dante.

"No, Dante, not now." Edward groaned. "Go fetch!"

The pines cast long shadows eastward across the rolling hills. It was late now, evening already, and they were both tired, hungry, and too lazy to move.

"We should get going," Edward said, lying flat on his back.

"I know," Jamie answered, her head cradled on his belly, one hand tossed up across his warm chest.

"It must be six, six-thirty."

"I don't know. I forgot to wear my watch."

"Me too."

The wind had picked up, tossing the tops of the pines. Dante lay at Edward's feet. At the sound of their voices, his heavy tail thumped, flattening pine needles.

"Why did you name him Dante?" Jamie asked.

Edward didn't answer for a moment. Then he said softly, "Because he accompanied me through several levels of hell."

Jamie felt a pain stab her heart. She rolled onto her side, her cheek against his bare chest. "Oh, Edward, I'm sorry. I forgot for the moment that there was anything but here and now."

He touched her cheek. "There isn't."

Riding home, Jamie was again in the lead. She had to hold tight to the reins to keep the chestnut from breaking into a gallop. The poor horse was starving . . . or at least putting on a good show.

"Much further?" she called over her shoulder.

Edward trotted up alongside. "Pardon?"

"I was just asking if we were almost there. I think my horse could eat a horse right now!"

Edward laughed. "Just another couple of miles. The house will be there, waiting for us, as we climb up over this ridge."

Jamie shook her head, amazed. "How is it possible, Edward?"

He didn't have to ask what she meant. "I don't know," he said. "I don't know how you could have painted my house, how your painting could connect with my carefully kept secret. It's one of life's mysteries, unexplainable—"

"Like the Bermuda Triangle and UFOs." She grinned.

"And 'Who was that masked man, anyway?' " he teased back.

"Wait! I know the answer to that one!" Jamie insisted, leaning toward him, but he laughed, kicking his horse to a gallop. "Later. In the tub! Now I'll race you back!"

He gave the black horse its head, riding smoothly up over the shoulder of the hill. With a whoop, Jamie took off after him. She could! She did! It was amazing. Nothing was impossible for her today, nothing!

TEN

Two people did indeed fit in the old claw-footed tub.

Edward climbed in first, all lean and muscled and gorgeous. Glancing over his shoulder as he stepped in, he caught Jamie admiring his buns. "Hey"—he laughed—"cut that out!"

"I can't help myself. You're irresistible and I can't be held responsible for my actions."

"Come in here with me," he coaxed, "and I'll hold you responsible, all right." His grin was wide, wicked, and utterly contagious.

Jamie let the robe she was wearing slip down off her shoulders, but she held one edge in front of her as she tiptoed to the tub. "I don't know," she drawled, "maybe the water's too hot."

"No," he answered solemnly, leaning back like a cat stretching.

"Too cold?" she whispered, her tongue darting over her lips.

"Uh-uh." Edward shook his head, his eyes locked on hers.

"You mean it's just right? Well, I'd better check for myself." Leaning down, she slipped her fingers into the water, then skated them across the surface to his chest . . . and on down his chest to his belly.

His lips parted and his breathing grew ragged. The magic leaped between them, from dark eyes to gray eyes, from smile to smile, from fingertips to skin. Was it only the exciting unfamiliarity of each other's body? The newness? The thrill?

Too dizzy to think, she rested her hands on his wet shoulders and looked deep into his dark and burning eyes.

Curving his free hand around her head, Edward drew her face down to his and kissed her. "Come on in here with me, Jamie. You've got goose bumps."

"I'm not a bit cold," she whispered.

"Then I'll take it as a compliment."

Smiling, Jamie let the robe fall to the floor and stepped into the tub, settling down in the space he made for her between his thighs.

Leaning her head back against his chest, she smiled. "This is quite nice, Mr. Rockford."

In answer he pressed his lips to the nape of her neck and nibbled there happily.

Shivers walked her skin. She giggled.

"You do that a lot," Edward whispered in her ear, his teeth closing oh so gently on her tender lobe.

"What?" she asked, all breathless and shaky.

"That. That giggle," he answered, snaking his tongue into the curve of her ear.

She pulled her shoulder up high, laughing and ducking out of his reach. "Me? Giggle? Never! If there's one thing I've assuredly never been known to do, not even as a tiny child, it's giggle."

"Then what do you call this?" he demanded, sliding his hands around over her wet and slippery ribs.

She squirmed and giggled, slapping at his hands. "Stop! Stop that!" She laughed. "Okay, I give! I admit it, under the *most* unusual . . ." She turned onto her knees, slipped her arms around his neck and kissed him. ". . . the *most* unexpected . . ." She kissed him again. ". . . the *most* unexplainable circumstances, I suppose I do giggle."

"And I love it. It's a sweet sound, Jamie Payton."

"And you're a sweet man, Edward Rockford. Sweet and delicious." She planted a kiss on his chest, right above his heart. And as her lips lingered there, drinking in the taste of him, the phone rang.

They both jumped.

The sound so startled her that the only recognizable emotion Jamie could feel was anger. "What the heck?"

Edward flinched as if he'd been struck from behind. His brows swooped low and his eyes darkened. He cocked his head, listening to the insistent ringing, but other than that, he didn't move a muscle. He was tense and taut as a wire, the sound of the phone vibrating along every nerve in his body.

When it was quiet, Jamie whispered, "Who could that be? I thought no one even knows about this place."

"No one does." He ran a hand back through his wet black hair. "No. But I left so many important things on hold, the office in chaos . . . I put my apartment phone on call forward. Anyone calling thinks they are trying there. But they had instructions to call only in an emergency."

"Oh, Edward." Jamie frowned, wavering between disappointment and anger. "It can't be that important. I mean, they hung up, right?"

"Right," he answered, leaning up against her so that his chest pressed against her breasts as he kissed her. "Right. So don't worry about it."

"I'm not worried," she answered, a frown belying her words. "I just thought this was really a hideaway. I didn't expect anyone to bother us."

"And no one will."

"Promise?"

It was Edward's turn to frown. "Jamie—"

"Say you promise. Say it!"

"Jamie, I promise to try my damnedest not to let anything interfere with this weekend."

"Oh!" She snorted in disdain and tossed her head. "That's a cop-out if I ever heard one."

"It is not," he insisted, catching her shoulders in his hands and trying to make her face him.

But Jamie was slippery as a fish. In one second she had scooted to the far end of the tub and sat with her knees drawn up to her chest, her arms wrapped around them. Without meeting his eyes, she snapped, "Hand me a towel, please."

"Jamie—" There was an edge to his voice suddenly, but she was past caring.

"I asked for a towel. Please."

"Get it yourself."

Head held high, she stepped from the tub and sauntered over to the towel rod behind his back. She was wrapping the huge terry-cloth bath sheet around her when the phone rang again.

She stopped, her hands pressed to her chest.

Standing, Edward met her gaze, his eyes as darkly troubled as hers.

Everything inside Jamie turned to water. "Please, Edward, don't answer it. We're so happy here. It's so wonderful. It's perfect. Please . . . don't ruin it."

In answer he came and folded her in his arms. He held her tightly against the solid wall of his chest until the phone stopped ringing. Then he smiled down at her. But behind the smile, deep in his dark eyes, shadows lurked.

Jamie tore her eyes away, pressing her cheek to his wet shoulder and hugging him as tightly as she could. "Thank you, Edward.

Thank you. And you won't be sorry." She looked up and forced a little laugh. "You know what? I'll cook you something wonderful for dinner and we can go walking in the moonlight and sit in front of that lovely fire—"

Instead, Edward cooked salmon on the outside grill and then they made love slowly, rapturously in his big oak bed. Jamie fell asleep in his arms, exhausted and peaceful.

Edward lay there, emotions warring across his handsome face. Outside the wind picked up, signaling a change in weather. There'd be a storm tomorrow for sure. And as he lay there he could sense it moving nearer, circling closer and closer to the house in the woods. He tightened his arm around the sleeping woman at his side but didn't look at her. Let her sleep. Let his unease not reach out and trouble her dreams. Tomorrow he would deal with tomorrow.

The phone woke them both in the morning. Groggy, disoriented, Edward reached for the phone, knocking it off the night table and onto the floor. Groping for the receiver, he brought it to his ear. "Yes?"

The voice at the other end, civil and polite though it was, snapped him back to reality.

The conversation was short and businesslike. Jamie caught only the good-bye.

When he hung up, Edward turned to face her.

She was snuggled down in the covers, her wide gray eyes open and questioning.

He didn't mince words. "That was the network president. They're having a cocktail party for the ambassador from Holland this evening. It's Dutch TV that I've been negotiating with these last months, the Dutch representative I left hanging this weekend, and my presence is essential. But it only means we have to leave a little earlier than I planned this afternoon."

Jamie looked away. It had to end sometime. She knew that. She'd always known that. All this was only a dream, a fantasy. "Okay," she said listlessly. "I understand."

Her acquiescence surprised and worried him. An idea leaped to his tongue before he could give it any thought. "Come with me, Jamie. It will be elegant, charming . . . one of those typical embassy affairs. Don't make me face it alone."

"No. Absolutely not." She ducked under the covers, her mind flooded with vivid, long-buried images: there she was, all dressed up in party clothes, standing next to the cold, disapproving shape of her father, and the instant before he paraded her out in front of his guests, he found fault with something: her clothes, her hair, the look on her face. Oh, he would destroy her with a word. . . .

She was so upset she could barely hear Edward's next words. He, of course, thought she was merely being stubborn. He tugged the corner of the blanket off her face and held her shoulder just tight enough to keep her from turning away.

"Come on, Jamie Payton . . . my friend, my lover. Come with me. We won't stay long. I have to put in an appearance, mingle a bit, charm the ambassador, apologize to the network rep. That's all. That's not so much to ask."

She bit at her lips, eyes lowered, all gloom and dismay.

"Please?" he coaxed, leaning down so his breath was warm on her cheek. "Come with me, Jamie. You'll be my alibi. One look at you and they'll understand why I disappeared without any explanation." He kissed her, rubbing his rough cheek against her tender skin. "They'll envy me instead of condemning me. Say yes, Jamie. Say yes—"

"Fine. All right." She yielded with as much grace as she could muster, but inside, deep inside, was an ember of unhappiness that needed only the slightest breeze to fan it into a blaze.

ELEVEN

Edward pulled up in front of Jamie's building and killed the engine. "Shall I wait here or come up while you change?" he asked, one arm hooked over the back of the seat.

"Why don't you go on to your place, get ready, and then come back and pick me up?"

He shook his head slowly, the corners of his mouth pulled down in a knowing grin. "Oh no, not a chance. If I let you out of my sight, you'll disappear on me."

"That's crazy," she objected hotly.

"Oh. Right. Tell me the thought never crossed your mind, Ms. Payton, not once on this long, silent ride home."

"Never mind." She slid out of the passenger seat and headed up the front steps.

Edward caught up and held the door for

her, then followed her up the six flights of stairs. In the loft, he leaned back against the door and crossed his arms over his chest to wait.

Jamie glowered at him, then grabbed a black silk dress from the closet along with a handful of other things and marched into the bathroom.

While she was gone Edward walked over to the easel and looked at her painting of his home. He stood there, staring at it, mesmerized. How was it possible? How could it be?

But then . . . was it any stranger than the fact that he was standing here, waiting for the woman he loved, missing her even for these few moments apart? How was *that* possible? It was unbelievable, incomprehensible.

"You!" he said, tapping the painting roughly, "It's all your fault. All part and parcel of the same magic. I don't understand, I may *never* understand, but there's not a damn thing I can do about it. The die is cast. *C'est un fait accompli.*"

"Who are you talking to?" Jamie asked, emerging from the bathroom.

"No one," Edward answered quickly.

"And in French, no less?"

"Never mind. Let's talk about you," he

said, smiling as he walked toward her. "You look beautiful."

"Do I?" she asked, looking down at herself in her little black dress, her black sheer stockings and heels. "You're sure?"

"Oh, my darling, you look *very* beautiful. And very sexy." He leaned over and kissed her neck. "Alluring. Captivating." He punctuated each word with a kiss until she pushed him away, laughing.

"Okay, okay. You've made your point, thank you," she retorted, and then her eyes met his. She smiled softly, a real smile, the first in hours, then said it again. "Thank you, Edward."

"You're welcome, Jamie. It's only the truth."

Holding out his arm like some Victorian gentleman, he waited for her to loop her hand through and then led her to the door. "It will be a lovely evening, you'll see."

An hour later, at dusk, they pulled up in front of one of Washington's elegant small hotels in the embassy district. The doorman helped her out of the car; the valet whisked the car away. There wasn't anything to do but take Edward's hand and walk at his side into the ballroom.

There were crystal chandeliers, ice sculptures, diamonds. The whole room glittered.

"Oh, I'm underdressed," Jamie whispered, pressing against Edward's solid bulk.

"Nonsense." He smiled down at her. "You're the most beautiful woman in the room." And the next minute they were engulfed by a crowd of strangers, shaking hands, smiling, nodding, exchanging small talk. A waiter sailed by like a tall ship, and the next thing Jamie knew she was holding a glass of champagne, sipping at the pale amber fizz. It went straight to her head. Things felt better. She could breathe again.

And here was the Dutch ambassador, every inch the elegant statesman, in tails no less, kissing her hand. How delightful! What *had* she been afraid of?

And then a movement at her side, a voice in her ear . . . a voice that brought the whole glittering charade crashing down in ruins.

Her father.

She jumped back, knocking Edward's drink down his shirtfront, but all she could do was stare at the man who stood there, smiling at her.

"What a surprise, Jamie. You are most certainly the last person I expected to see here."

"Father! I . . . I—"

"She is here with me, Mr. Payton. I'm Edward Rockford. We've met before, but—"

"Oh, I remember you quite well, Mr. Rockford. We met at the Northern European trade talks, am I correct?"

"Yes, quite right." As he spoke Edward managed to slip an arm around Jamie's waist and then, on the pretense of reaching for a new drink, he stepped between father and daughter and stood there, solid, protecting.

But for Jamie it was as if he were made of glass. Her father's shadow filled the room, reaching around Edward and the other guests to find her, assault her.

When her father turned his attention toward a passing tray of hors d'oeuvres, Edward leaned down and whispered, "Tough it out, Jamie. Show him up. Remember, you can always tell him to stuff it."

James Payton sank his teeth into the tiny mound of caviar while his eyes, cold as a snake's, flicked across Jamie's face. But his words were directed to the man at his daughter's side. "Edward . . . You don't mind if I call you Edward, do you?"

"Not at all, James."

"Good." The older man smiled. "Edward, so how long have you known my daughter?"

Jamie saw red. Here she was, standing right here, and he was giving her no more respect than he had when she was ten. Tossing back the rest of her champagne, she handed the empty glass to Edward. "Could you get me a refill, please?"

A hint of a smile played across Edward's mouth. With a small nod he excused himself as Jamie spun toward her father. "If you want to know anything about me—which would be a first—you can damn well ask me."

He gave her a conciliatory smile, couched in his usual arrogance, and glanced at Edward's retreating back. "I was only going to say that you finally have shown some good sense, my dear. That young man is someone to be reckoned with. He's astute, bold . . . a real mover and shaker." His eyes swung back to her face. "You surprised me, that's all. Surprised and pleased me."

Uncontrollably, her heart leaped.

But then, with a careless shrug, he took it all back. "Of course, your choice of apparel shows your usual lack of savoir faire."

Jamie gasped. The room spun and she went with it. Turning, she brushed against one couple then another, racing for the doorway.

Edward caught her just inside. "Slow down. Walk, Jamie, just hold up your head and walk out. Slowly. It's okay. I'm here with you."

In the lobby she leaned against a wall next to a tall potted ficus. Her hands were shaking. She had to blink to keep from crying.

"I am so sorry, Jamie. I had no idea—"

"It's not your fault. I'm fine, really. You can just go back in and I'll take a cab."

"Don't be silly."

"No. Don't *you* be silly," she said, flicking a tongue over dry lips. "This is business. It's important for you. Go back in and—"

"Forget it, Jamie," he answered harshly, taking hold of her arm. "I'll take you home."

"But I don't want you to take me home!"

People turned, then quickly slid their eyes away.

Jamie felt her eyes sting with tears. She hated this! Oh, she hated this whole thing, the embarrassment, the helplessness, the uncontrollable feelings. She hated it all.

When Edward tipped her face up to his, that was what he saw.

The look in her eyes made him drop his hand. He drew in a deep, uneasy breath. "Jamie, whatever he said—"

"Do you want to know what he said?" she

hissed. "He said that being here with you was the first thing I ever did right in my whole life!"

Edward grimaced, closed his eyes. "Oh, Jamie—"

"Don't look so upset. *You* should be happy. He likes you. He *admires* you." Her voice absolutely dripped with sarcasm. "He thinks you're a worthy adversary, someone worth paying attention to, someone who can *demand* his attention—"

"Enough, Jamie. That's enough," he snapped.

Jamie pressed her lips together and lifted her chin. "I'm going home."

"And I'm taking you." He stalked to the door at her side, then took her arm and handed the valet the stub.

He glanced over at her, hoping, wishing for some response on her part, but it was like standing next to a statue. She only moved when the car slid to a stop in front of them and the valet opened the door.

Jamie sank into the seat and sat there, her hands folded in her lap.

Edward slid in behind the wheel. "Can I take you to my place, Jamie? We can talk. I'll order something in for dinner."

"I'm not hungry, thank you. And I want to go home."

"Will you let me in?"

She stared out the window.

"Jamie, will you let me in?" And suddenly there were emotions churning there, naked and raw. For Jamie it was like looking down into a roomful of snakes.

She shook her head. "I just want to go home. I want to be by myself for a while. Please, Edward. Please?"

"But why are you so angry at me? Tell me."

"Because you took me there."

"But that doesn't make any sense; you said so yourself. I had no idea he'd be there. I didn't plan it. It just happened."

" 'It just happened,' " Jamie echoed, shaking her head. "We seem to be saying that a lot lately, you and I. The trouble is, I don't like things that 'just happen.' I like things to be nice and predictable. Safe. Sensible."

"So do I, but that's not how the world works."

"It's how it *used to work.*" She glared at him and he held her gaze, anger and confusion snapping between them like electricity.

Finally he shook his head and looked away

out through the windshield. "I'll take you home. We'll talk about it another day."

"Fine," she said, sitting stiff and upright. She was stone; she didn't feel a thing. She didn't have to talk, she didn't have to think, she didn't have to feel anything.

"There's something else, isn't there?" he said, his voice cold and distant now. "What is it? Why else are you so angry with me?"

What could she say? Could she tell him that if her father, whom she hated, whom she distrusted, whom she despised more than anything on earth at that moment . . . if he could look so favorably on this man at her side, then something must be wrong? Could she say that? Could she explain it?

But the thought gnawed at her heart. Something must be wrong. She had missed it. She had been blind. She had been foolish. It was her mistake . . . and better to correct it now than pay for it later.

She blinked hard, but the tears spilled over anyway and slid down her cheeks. She kept her face turned away and didn't make a sound. When Edward stopped the car and got out in front of her place, she quickly wiped her face on her arm and got out before he could offer his hand.

"Good night, Edward. Please, don't come up. I'll . . . I'll talk to soon."

"When?"

"I don't know. Soon. I'll call you."

"Will you?"

"Yes. Of course."

"Oh, Jamie—" he whispered, and there was pain in his voice, pain warring with sorrow and confusion.

It brought her eyes up to his face. She shook her head, her eyes brimming again with tears. She had to look down, look away. "Oh." With one trembling finger, she touched the front of his shirt, the crisp white loveliness stained with champagne.

"I'm sorry, Edward. I am really so sorry. I didn't mean for it to happen. Not any of it! I'm sorry!"

But when he tried to pull her to him, to press her against his chest, she ran into the building and was gone.

Long after even the echo of her footsteps had died, Edward stood there at the door, the door that was closed against him. It was like standing in the pits of hell. He felt as if all light, all happiness had been snatched away from him again. Again!

A sudden wild impulse shook him, a need to smash his hand through the door, to cry and curse, to howl at the moon. But not he. Certainly not here in the open, on some busy city street. Never.

Clenching his teeth, he wiped a hand over his face and stepped back. He would wait. He would give her the time and space she needed. He would pay her the courtesy of letting her be the one to make the next move. He would do that. He could. He *could* . . .

. . . because he had to. He no longer had a choice. Even if he could convince his mind that there were any options, his heart would not be swayed. For him, it was already written in the book of fate: this woman, and this woman only, forever.

TWELVE

Three days later Edward broke that promise to himself. He could not wait for Jamie to make the first move; he had to call her. He closed the door to his office, told his secretary to hold all calls, and picked up the phone. He sat there for a moment, holding the phone in his lap, trying to decide what words to use. Surely there were words that would convince Jamie, words that would reach her, words that would touch her. He just had to find the right ones.

Nothing came. Not one clear thought, not one sensible idea.

It had been that way since he last saw her. He felt cut off from everything, disconnected, adrift, lost. But now necessity ruled. He had to fly to Amsterdam to complete these negotiations and he was damn well not leaving the country without seeing her, without at least speaking to her.

Anger powered him. He dialed, held the receiver to his ear, counted the rings. Circles of sweat grew under his arms and his shirt stuck to his back. Climbing a mountain was easier than this. Roping a horse. Putting together a multimillion-dollar deal. Anything!

On the ninth ring, just as he was about to give up, Jamie picked up the phone. "Hello?"

Edward rubbed at the pain above his eyes. He took a breath. "Hello, Jamie. It's me. I know you didn't want me to call. I know you wanted some time to think—"

"It's all right. How are you?"

Did she sound concerned? More than that? Less? His heart ached with the need to know. But he pitched his voice low, calm and dispassionate.

"I'm okay. You?"

"I'm fine." A pause, a silence he could not read. Then her lovely voice, but cool and distant. "I've been busy with a painting. Something new I'm trying. A still life. Actually you caught me right in the middle of working—"

"I'm sorry. I was going to wait until I heard from you—"

"I thought that was what we agreed."

"Yes. I know. But I have to leave. I have to fly to Amsterdam for work. I could be gone a week or more. I . . ." He shook his head, pressing his fingers to his temples. Eyes closed, he went on. "I didn't want to leave without seeing you. We need to talk."

"When do you leave?"

His heart took a little leap. "Not until tomorrow morning. I've got a nine A.M. flight."

"Oh."

He waited, fingers crossed, but she quickly destroyed even that glimmer of hope.

"It turns out I'm going to visit a friend of mine this afternoon, over in Maryland, and I won't be back until tomorrow night. . . . I'm sorry."

Damn! She was not going to make this easy, was she?

"What friend?" he demanded. "I didn't know you had a friend in Maryland. Where in Maryland?"

"In Olney." She laughed softly, but even that sweet sound was quickly curbed. "Edward, there are many things you don't know about me. Really, you hardly know me at all—"

"I *love* you." It was out before he could stop the words. "And I *do* know you, I know you're frightened and unhappy and determined not to feel anything. I know that. And I understand it. And if I had all the time in the world, I'd give you the luxury of saying no for as long as you want before you finally realize that you love me, too, damm it, and what you really want to say is yes. 'Yes. I love you too.' That's what you want to say! But instead we've got to work our way through all of this, goddammit—"

"Edward, you're yelling. You're yelling at me, and I won't listen to it."

"I'm coming over. This instant. Wait for me."

"I was just leaving—"

"You said you were painting. So wait for me. Give me ten minutes, five minutes to talk to you—"

"I can't. I'll miss the train. I'll be late. I have to go—"

"Jamie, wait for me!"

He slammed down the phone, grabbed his suit jacket, and stormed out the door.

"Mr. Rockford! You've got a call on three, and someone waiting outside—"

"Take care of it. I'll be back later."

He flagged a cab and rode crosstown, leaning far forward, staring out the windshield, urging the car to go faster with every muscle and fiber of his being. He had the door open even before the cab rolled to a stop. "Thanks. Keep the change."

He took the steps two at a time, one flight after another.

When he reached the sixth-floor landing, Jamie was just coming out of the loft, duffel bag in hand.

He stood at the top of the stairs, blocking her way, an immovable obstacle seething with anger and despair. "You weren't going to wait for me?"

"I . . . I told you . . . I have to make a train."

"To Olney."

"Yes," she snapped, dropping the duffel and folding her arms across her chest.

"Jamie, don't do this. I know you're afraid. I understand."

"Great. That's wonderful, Edward. I'm really glad. Because I like you and I want us to be friends—"

"Friends? *I love you.* No, don't interrupt and *don't* turn away. I love you, Jamie Payton, and I know you love me! I know that, here—" He slapped his chest hard with the flat of one hand. "And all the rest, we'll work it out. We'll banish the sadness, the fear, all those bad feelings you won't, or can't, talk about. We'll—"

"What do you think you are? A magician? One wave of your magic wand and everything's just fine and dandy?"

He narrowed his eyes but kept them riveted to her face, thinking, wondering. "What makes you so angry with me when what I'm offering is happiness?"

"Your arrogance! Your damn conceit!"

"Mine? Me?" He groaned, spreading his arms wide. "Jamie, if there's one thing I have not felt through all of this, it's the least bit sure of myself. For once, for the first time in ten years, I'm way out here, balancing on a tightrope, way up in space, and I haven't got a net."

She blinked, then pulled her eyes away from his face. "Well, you sound arrogant. You sound—" She let it drop, shrugging her shoulders in hopeless resignation.

"What?" he asked, opening his hands. "What? Like your father?"

"Exactly!" She snapped her eyes back to his face. "You sound like you know all the answers. What I should be doing, what I shouldn't—"

"*So that's it.* Oh, I should have guessed. Well, I'll tell you something, Jamie. I am *not* like your father. I am not *one bit* the same kind of man that he is. I don't like him. And I am sorry that we saw him, and that in some stupid way he made you think that he likes me. He doesn't. He doesn't even *know* me. And"—he leaned toward her, his dark eyes burning, fierce and passionate—"as far as knowing all the answers, well, I don't. I'm as confused as you are, except . . ." He whispered, breathing hard, "Except for one thing—I know we love each other, and one way or another, we *will* be happy!"

Jamie shook her head, her lips quivering. "You just don't get it. I don't want to be that happy, because I can't stand being unhappy. I can't. I can't take any more. I want things to be simple, ordinary, manageable, the way they used to be."

She bent and picked up her duffel and held it to her chest. "Edward, you're going away tomorrow. I . . . I think that's good. We'll both have time to think, to get our bearings. You can get all involved in business again, and I can paint. It will be good for us."

"Not for me." His eyes were wet, vulnerable, and tormented.

Jamie looked away. "Yes, it will. It will be okay. And I'll talk to you when you get back. You'll see—" She ducked under his arm and scooted down the stairs. From the landing below, her voice wafted up. "You'll see. It's better this way."

Jamie waited in the corner booth at the coffee shop until she saw Edward leave the building and walk away. Then she pushed away her untasted cup of coffee, went back to the loft, and lifted the receiver off the hook.

She sat for a moment, the phone in her lap, looking at the wall. A thousand thoughts whirled and clashed inside her head, a broken kaleidoscope that could not come into focus. All she wanted to do was sleep. It was really all she had done for the past three days.

A canvas sat on the easel, the basic outline of a still life . . . and everywhere, covering every empty space, were faint pencil sketches of a man's face, a dark, handsome, familiar face.

With a sharp cry, Jamie threw her shoe at it, knocking the whole thing to the floor. Then she dropped onto the bed and pulled the covers over her head.

THIRTEEN

For an entire day Jamie hid from herself, from the world, from whoever it was who came knocking on her door calling "Delivery!" She didn't trust anyone, most certainly not *herself*. She felt incapable of making the smallest decision. She felt worn-out and used up. At the same time she felt as if she were a child again, stuck in the past, trapped at the most miserable point of her life. But she was helpless to do anything about it.

Necessity would have to move her. Fate would have to intervene.

And slowly, step-by-step, it did.

It started with a simple trip to the store. She had to go because she was out of milk and coffee and her bread was sprouting a furry green crust. Besides that, her attempts at painting were hideous; she couldn't bear to look at them. So a trip to the grocery store seemed like a safe bet.

She made it back in under an hour to find her neighbor, Kent, waiting for her at the top of the stairs. Actually he didn't even wait for her to get that far.

"Jamie?" he called down. "Is that you? Hurry up! I've got a surprise for you."

Great. Jamie groaned, kicking at each step as she made her way up the last flight. Just what I need!

She found him standing outside his door, his arms full of roses. Pink roses.

"There's more inside," he sputtered, overcome with amazement. "Take a look in there! I mean, it's hard to believe there are this many roses in the whole world. And all of them pink! Have you ever seen so many gorgeous pink roses?"

Jamie could only shake her head dumbly as he piled the flowers in her arms, then raced inside to get the rest of them. "These are fantastic flowers! I mean it, Jamie, you must have some admirer."

She bent her head into the midst of all that pink sweetness and took a breath.

Kent was talking again. "You should have seen the delivery boy. The kid made it up all six flights of stairs and almost passed out. I happened to be on my way down for the mail and saw it. There he was, slumped in front of your door, knocking and cursing. He said he had been here yesterday, up and down, carrying all these roses, and he was damned if he was going to take 'em back again. I said I'd be glad to help. . . . Keep them, I mean, not carry them!" He laughed, pleased as punch with his role in the whole affair. Then he frowned. "I hope that was okay?"

Jamie collected her wits and answered politely, "Oh, yes. Thank you, Kent. That was very nice of you."

"Anytime! Just call on me, your friendly neighborhood—"

"Thanks, Kent. Bye."

"Hey, don't you want me to carry these in for you? And the groceries?"

Jamie blushed. "Yes, of course. Thanks."

He followed her in and then turned, holding the roses, looking for a place to put them.

Jamie followed his glance around the near-empty room, the clutter in the corner that passed for a kitchen, the scattered canvases, the worn sofa that was about all the furniture she owned. There wasn't much there.

Their eyes met and Kent grinned. "You're

kind of a gypsy like me, huh? Just passing through."

He turned before he saw the pained look that washed across Jamie's face. Laying the roses on the table, he headed for the door. "See ya. And remember, just knock if you need anything."

"Yes. Thank you," she whispered.

She felt light-headed and weak-kneed. If she had been given to that kind of thing, she would have fainted. Instead she hugged the roses to her chest and fought back her tears. When she could manage it, she pulled an old glass pitcher out of a cabinet and set one bouquet in there. A small, sealed gift enclosure fluttered to the floor.

With shaking fingers, Jamie lifted the point of the envelope and drew out the tiny white card.

> If roses can bloom, why not happiness? Why not love? Please call me, Jamie, or put your phone back on the hook so I can call you. Please. I love you.
>
> Edward

His phone number in Amsterdam was written on the bottom.

Jamie backed away until she bumped into

the sofa. She sat down, holding the card, trying to sort through her emotions. It was like trying to unravel a huge knot, a thousand threads all tangled together: her father, her childhood, the way she felt about her parents, about herself, the questions that Edward raised, always raised, *insisted* on raising. "Why won't he just leave well enough alone?" she cried aloud.

Angrily she flipped the card into the air. A breeze caught it and carried it across the room, then dropped it next to the phone and its disconnected plug. Jamie stared, the breath sucked out of her lungs. "Oh . . . great!" she whispered. "Omens, now? What's next? Portents? Oracles? Crystal balls? Oh, if I had a friend, in Olney or anywhere, I'd call her now."

At ten the next morning there was a loud knock on the door, like the hand of fate. "Delivery!"

Jamie dropped the pencil she was sketching with and stepped to the door. Leaving the chain lock on, she peeked out. Sure enough, there was a delivery person, a girl this time, dressed in shorts and high-top purple sneakers. "Hi! I have a delivery for Ms. Jamie Payton."

"Yes. One moment, please." She slipped the lock and opened the door. The girl dropped an enormous box into her arms. "Oh, wait. Sign here." She traded clipboard for box, then back again, and went clattering down the stairs.

Jamie stood there, but when Kent opened his door and poked his head out, she disappeared like a turtle into its shell. Leaning back against the door, she shook her head. "Stop! Stop this, Edward! It's foolish. It's silly—"

But not all the self-control in the world could keep her from opening the package. She had to; it was irresistible.

Inside the large shipping box was a smaller one wrapped in an elegant and distinctive floral paper, a small gold seal affixed at the bottom of a luscious satin bow. Inside, wrapped in layers of tissue, was a scarf, the most beautiful scarf Jamie had ever seen. Vibrant, lush, earthy, and mystical at the same time, the design delighted her artist's eye. The fabric itself was weightless, woven of moonbeams and starlight . . . or so it seemed. And so it felt, draped across her shoulders. She lifted one shoulder, rubbing her cheek against its perfect warmth and softness, and at once she felt the touch of Edward's hand, a dream of a touch from far away.

Magic.

Oh my! Her breath flew away. How should she act? What should she do? What would happen next?

She didn't have a clue . . . until Karl Viereck, the gallery owner, knocked on her door.

"Finally!" he said, breezing past her into the loft. "So, where is it? Where is that painting? I am taking it with me now, this moment, and I will brook no argument. I was telling an excellent customer about this new work of yours and he is very interested. *Very* interested. He wants to see it this afternoon. With luck, I will have a check for you within a week. And, my dear girl"—he kissed her cheek and headed for the door—"if you will paint me some more like this, with this power and this passion, I will sell them all as quickly. I may make you famous despite yourself. And Jamie—eat something; you're looking very pale."

Then he was gone.

Jamie was flabbergasted. She didn't know what to do next. But with the landscape gone, the loft felt hollow and soulless. At least she could do something about *that.*

All afternoon and evening she worked on a

new painting . . . and as she hoped, *as she dreamed*, there beneath the abstract was another landscape: Edward's landscape, his trees, his house, his door. She gave herself up to the painting and found herself depicting autumn leaves, smoke from the chimney, the shadow of the unseen barn falling across the ground and carrying with it the promise of warm horses and sweet hay. The season was turning, time moving swiftly on the canvas. How? Why?

Jamie had no answers, only the need to paint. She kept at it until she was running out of paints and energy both. Then she fell asleep on the couch, her head on one arm, wrapped in the shawl with its ends knotted over her breasts. And she dreamed of Edward, a veiled, erotic dream in which she kissed him, touched him, felt him touching her.

In the morning she sat on the floor, the box of paints on her lap. She needed more . . . and more than that, she needed some answers. This was making her crazy. She checked inside the lid for a business label, an address, but there was nothing. She turned the whole box upside down, spilling wrinkled tubes in all directions, but there was nothing on the bottom either.

Stubbornness seized her. She might not be

able to figure out her life, but she could damn well solve this little mystery—

That was it! *The sign.* Hadn't there been a sign outside that old shop, a worn old sign whose remaining letters spelled *mystery* or *mysterious* or something like that? Think, Jamie Payton, think!

Biting her lip, Jamie called information but got no further than, "I'm sorry, but without the correct spelling or street address, I'm afraid I can't help you."

Dressed hurriedly in jeans and a T-shirt, she knocked on Kent's door.

"I need a favor. May I borrow your phone book? I spilled turpentine on mine months ago and it's ruined."

"Sure," he said, rubbing his eyes. "I'll get it for you. You wanna come in?"

"No. And I woke you, didn't I? I'm sorry. I wasn't thinking—"

"No sweat. Here, can I help?"

Jamie was already flipping through the pages, trying to balance the heavy book in one hand. She ran her finger down all the business listings under *M*, then turned to the Yellow Pages under *antiques*. Frowning, she tried *art supplies* with just as little success. "Damn!"

"Can I help?"

She looked at him without seeing him; her

wide gray eyes were focused somewhere far away. "What else could I look under for . . . well, just a collection of strange things?"

He shrugged. "Antiques?"

"Tried it."

"Okay." He screwed up his face in concentration. "How about *collectibles* . . . *curios* . . . *pawnshops* . . . *secondhand stores*. . . *junk*?"

She tried each one, then closed the book with a groan. "Nothing. And we're headed in the wrong direction. The stuff was . . . well, it was stranger than that. The whole shop was stranger than that. There was something . . . I don't know—"

"What?" He shrugged, blinking like an owl.

"Something mystical about it."

"Yeah, sure." He laughed. Then he saw the look on her face. "You're not pulling my leg, are you? Well then, try *magic* . . . Not there either? Okay, try *theatrical supplies*. . . . No? Sorry, but I'm out of ideas."

Disappointment filled Jamie. She handed him back the book. "Thanks anyway," she said softly.

"What is it?" he asked. "Someplace you've been before?"

She nodded.

"Then why not just go over?"

She got that faraway look again. "I happened upon it. I don't know if I could find it again."

"I'll help. Come on, don't say no so fast. Let me help. I haven't got rehearsal until two and I don't mind. I can use the exercise."

"Thanks," she said. "That's really nice of you."

"Hey, it's my pleasure. Sometimes you just have to let people in, ya know?"

A memory flickered behind her dove-gray eyes. She looked away. "Can you be ready in ten minutes?"

"No problem; I'll be ready in five."

They walked the streets all morning and on past noon. Jamie was in the lead, and every once in a while she got the feeling that she was close, that she was almost there . . . but she never did find the little shop. She never even found the street.

At one o'clock she left Kent at the bus stop. "Thanks for coming along." She shrugged, forcing a little smile. "Sorry I wasted your day."

"It wasn't a waste; I enjoyed the walk . . . all twenty-six miles of it!" He laughed and waved as he climbed on the bus. "Besides, that's what friends are for."

She felt strangely moved by his remark, by both its casualness and sincerity. Was it that easy for other people? Reach out and there was someone waiting? Ask and someone would be there? Is this how it felt? Was this the first step, the baby step, that a person took to open up, to be free and caring and loving, to let someone in . . . ?

Suddenly she was bawling like a little kid, right there in the middle of the street, the tears just spilling out of her eyes and down her face. It was as though a storm of emotion had blown up inside her. There was no warning and no controlling it. Trembling, shaking, she fumbled in her pocket, found a tissue, and blew her nose. Oh, my God! What is happening to me? Ducking her head, she kept her eyes on the ground and hurried home.

In the loft she made herself a cup of hot chocolate. It was still seventy degrees outside, but hot chocolate was one of those things she always thought would make her feel better, like a teddy bear when she was little. Blowing on it, she watched the steam rise and in it were images, faces: her mother first, and then her father, rising, shifting, fading away; the strange old man from the shop, his face wreathed in smiles and smoke as it, too, faded; and then Edward's face, handsome and filled with passion, eager, daring, and demanding. Even as a shadow he wanted too much!

She spilled the chocolate down the drain and wiped her hands on the front of her jeans.

"Get a grip, woman!" she said out loud, her voice breaking the stillness that held the loft as in a spell. "Get to work. Do something useful."

She painted again, working on the landscape because she had no choice. She squeezed the tubes of paint dry, rolling them up from the bottom like tiny tubes of toothpaste, but so beautiful, the last drops of paint as vivid and bright and rich as when she had first unscrewed the little sealed tops. Palm open, she could hold eight, nine tubes in one hand: Prussian blue, alizarin crimson, pure white, lamp black, burnt sienna, ocher, cadmium yellow, cinnabar, Venetian red. On the canvas they leaped to life, warm and vibrant, glowing, yet subtle and deep . . . amazing. The painting itself was amazing, as the first had been. She could see it herself. It was marvelous. It was real.

Jamie put down the brush and walked to the window. It was growing dark out there. Night was approaching in Washington. In Amsterdam it would be very late already, past midnight, six hours later. But which was real?

Was it seven o'clock or was it already one in the morning? Was it today, or was it already tomorrow? Which *was* real? Was *anything* real?

And Edward . . . what was he doing? Was he sitting at a desk in some hotel there, reviewing his notes, writing up corporate plans? Was he in bed, asleep and dreaming, or lying there, with his eyes open, thinking? Of what? Of her? Was he lying there, one hand thrown over his bare chest, the other over his eyes, thinking about her, missing her, wanting her, needing her?

The thought was like a rough hand squeezing her heart, squeezing out every drop of emotion: confusion, bewilderment, desire, longing, fear, and love. She had never felt such pain before, and without thinking, she leaned out into the night and whispered his name. But she didn't know what else to say. There were words, there *had to be* words, but she couldn't find them, couldn't speak them.

She shut the window. Turned off the lights. And again she drifted into an uneasy sleep on the unmade sofa, with only the shawl for cover.

When someone knocked on her door in the middle of the night, she was awake instantly, her senses keen, expectant. She hurried to the door. Chain on, she opened it, peeked out, then shut it and slid the chain out of the lock.

"Hi," she whispered.

Edward Rockford was standing there, dark hair tousled, eyes bleary, a day's growth on his jaw. "Hi. I flew in from Amsterdam. I couldn't stand it any longer."

She held out her hand and drew him inside. "Here. Let me take your jacket."

"Thanks." He sank down onto the edge of the sofa, rubbing the back of his neck. "I woke you, didn't I? I'm sorry."

"It's okay. What time is it?"

"Three-thirty in the morning." He glanced at his watch. "Almost four. Sorry."

"It's okay. It's strange—"

"Don't I know it!"

She laughed softly. "I was going to say, it's strange, but I almost expected you."

"Did you?" he asked, standing and moving close to her. "Did you want me to come?"

She looked into his eyes, those eyes that held every promise in the world . . . and she looked away. "I don't know, Edward. I'd be lying to you if I said anything else."

"Oh, God forbid you should lie to me! No, what I need now is some good harsh reality. To hell with dreams, possibilities, hopes. We can't have any of that—"

"Edward, don't."

"Okay, okay, I'm sorry. Don't walk away, please. I'll be quiet. I'll be calm and rational, the very epitome of patience. Really. Truly. Please sit back down with me."

"I'm sitting."

"Will you sit closer?" A quick flash of that irrepressible brashness of his, and then he was serious again. "Jamie, we have to talk."

"I know," she answered, meeting his dark gaze. "I know. I just wanted some time to think first."

"That's what scares me."

She blinked. "Why?"

"Because you're letting your head completely rule your heart."

"Wait a minute. You're the one who told me he'd learned to look before he leaped, to be cautious, to be—"

"Yes, and look what it got me—ten bitter years of loneliness and despair. But no more, Jamie. No more! I've made peace with all that. What I did, I did out of love, and though it ended in grief, at least I tried. But the past is past, and now what I want is the present . . .

and the future. I want *you.* I love you. And the truth is, you love me—"

She stood. "What I love is how you make that leap for me. You just jump right in there and say it—"

"*You* said it once, in the heat of passion. Admit it now!"

She bit at her lower lip, her eyes flashing. "I'm not going to say anything I don't want to say."

"Oh, Jamie . . . whether you say it or not, I know it's true. I've held you; I've loved you; I've watched you sleep in my arms. I *know* you love me!"

"Fine. Then I admit it. I love you." She threw herself back down on the couch, her arms crossed over her chest.

"Thank you," he said softly, a smile tugging at the corners of his mouth. "That was worth flying nine hours for."

"Well, don't let it go to your head." She fought down a smile of her own, but it was hard work; his happiness was contagious, intoxicating. It scared her. "Edward, oh Edward, don't do this. Don't just leap right in there; let's talk. Please, try to listen, try to understand what I'm thinking."

"What I want to know is what you're feeling. Once. Now. Tell me. Open your heart.

Let me in. Don't hide behind words and that logic of yours—"

"But that's the point. I have to. I can't do it any other way."

"Can't or won't?" Now he was on his feet, leaning over her, his hands spread on the cushions at her sides, his face just inches from hers. "Trust me, Jamie. Take the chance. Grab at the gold ring. Trust me!"

She pressed her hands against the hard wall of his chest, pushing him away. "See, you're not listening to me. It's you, you, you . . . not me!"

He didn't budge. His eyes blazed into her soul. "It's *us*. It's the two of us together, through everything, for our whole lives. The two of us, connected, bound by love. Not either of us alone again. Listen to me, Jamie. Trust me!"

"I can't!" She slid out from under his arm and ran to the far side of the room. She was shaking and crying. "I can't, Edward. You're asking too much."

"Of course." He straightened, let his hands fall to his sides. "I know that, Jamie. I know how hard this is for you. But all I want is to love you. Like now, I want to gather you in my arms and let you cry there, safe and loved. I want to feel your tears on my skin just as I want to hear your laughter, smooth your frown, make you giggle like a little girl."

"But I'm not a little girl!" she snapped.

He closed his eyes, rubbed at his temples. "Oh. That old stuff, all that old stuff. You're letting the past haunt you, Jamie. You're letting it control your life."

"It's my life."

"It's our lives! Ours. *My* future as well as yours. I'm paying for your father's cruelty."

"Who's asking you to? Huh? And besides, you can just get out, walk away, leave me alone. No one's asking for your help. No one's asking you to do anything!"

"But I will. I will do anything, Jamie, *anything*. Just tell me what to do, what to say to prove to you that I am not like him. I won't hurt you. I won't!"

She turned away, crying.

He wrapped his arms around her from behind, pulled her into the warm circle of his arms. He could feel how she trembled. Her tears dropped onto his hands. "Oh, my darling," he whispered into her hair, "if I can't find the right words to convince you, then let my actions speak for me. Jamie . . . Jamie, look at me."

Gently he turned her toward him. "Jamie, look at me. I'm here. I've flown nine hours, four thousand miles, to be here . . . because I love you. I need you. I want you. *I love you.* And I'm here. Jamie, would your father ever have done that? Would he have crossed an ocean to be with your mother? Would he have put his emotions before his work? Would he have dropped everything to be with the ones who needed him, who loved him? Would he?"

When she didn't answer, he closed his eyes, shook his head. It was agony to hold her and have her give nothing in response. It was torture . . . absolute torture to be this close and feel her all cold and stubborn, locked away from him. "Say something, Jamie. For God's sake, say something! Answer me! Love me!"

"Edward, I *do* love you. You wanted me to say it and I did. But . . ." Her eyes looked like bruises in her sweet face. Her lips were quivering and there were tears on her cheeks. "But what good does it do? You want more than that now. And I can't give any more. I didn't even think I could give as much as I already have, and any more would just break me into pieces. I'm not strong enough. I'm not brave enough—"

"Jamie, dearest—"

"No! Don't push me! Do you hear me?

Do you hear what I'm saying? I am saying no, Edward. No!"

He stepped back. He searched her face, his own eyes bruised and tortured. "Don't, Jamie, don't do this. If you don't want to make a commitment now, we won't. If you won't marry me, then we'll go on as we are. It will be enough. Don't even say anything. Just come with me. Come back with me to Europe, Jamie."

She bit her lip, shook her head. "No, Edward. I can't."

He looked away. She could see his chest rise with the great shuddering intake of his breath. Then he faced her again, his self-control barely held in place. "I've got the corporate jet waiting for a six A.M. departure. I thought we'd be on it together, flying off into a future filled with happiness—" But his voice failed him. His broad shoulders lifted and fell as he struggled to contain his despair. "Call me, Jamie. Call me sometime, anytime." He turned his back to her and then his hand was on the door and the door was open. "I guess I'd better get to the airport."

Then there was only the empty doorway where he had stood waiting for one word from her to call him back. There was only silence.

FOURTEEN

It was six o'clock. At this very moment Edward's plane was taking off without her. Perhaps that was the realization that jolted her out of her stupor. *He was gone.*

Suddenly she realized what was happening, what she was feeling, and what it was that she didn't want to feel anymore. In one moment she went from a frightened child, battered and buffeted by years without love, to a woman who would make love happen . . . who would create her own destiny.

She would. She could. She had been offered love by a brave heroic man and she would be his equal, his match, his best friend and lover. Yes! Her heart was hers . . . not her father's, not her mother's, *hers.* Her spirit was hers; not some tattered little wisp of a thing but strong and billowing with hope, like a sail that could carry her anywhere. Her thoughts and wishes and dreams were her own to shape, and shape them she would, around the daring dreams of the man she loved.

Reaching for the phone, she heard nothing, a blank. Laughing giddily to herself, she plugged the cord back in the wall, waited for a dial tone, and then called information. "Delta Airlines, please. Thank you."

The first flight she could get a seat on was scheduled for departure at 12:55 that afternoon. She was on it, her seat belt fastened, her tray table in its upright and locked position, her coat stowed in the overhead compartment. She was so excited that her hands were shaking.

Passing by, the flight attendant gave her a reassuring smile. "Everything will be fine, dear. Relax."

Jamie almost laughed out loud.

She would have been laughing all the way to Amsterdam if the plane had ever gotten off the runway. It made it that far, but no farther.

Sitting there the first hour, she had plenty of time to plan her next moves. She'd arrive in Amsterdam at five-thirty tomorrow morning.

She'd dial his number, wake him up, and tell him she was there. She'd race over, leap into his bed, into his arms! Not a bad little scenario, right? And here she was, on her way.

Or she'd *be* on her way if this stupid plane would ever take off. Uh-oh! Never ever say anything bad about the plane you're about to fly in across a very large ocean. Overnight. In the dark.

"Sorry," she whispered, patting the arm of her seat.

"Getting impatient?" asked the woman to her left.

"A bit." Jamie smiled.

"Well, I'm sure it's nothing. We'll probably be off in a minute or two."

Another hour later they were still sitting there. Two whole hours of precious travel time had been wasted! By now she wanted to scream. The air inside the plane was stale and heavy. The free Cokes had melted to water. Her heart was pounding. Her nerves were strung tight as violin strings. She was going to cry.

The pilot's voice rasping over the intercom sounded as disgusted as she felt. "This is Captain Wagner in the cockpit. I am sorry for the delay, folks, but we have a problem with the rear exit. We're going to have to return to the gate and deplane. We do hope to be able to reboard in a couple of hours. Please listen for the announcement. Again, I apologize for this inconvenience. Thank you."

The cabin echoed with groans and moans as the plane taxied back to the gate. Jamie filed off with all the other disgruntled passengers. She flopped into a hard, round-backed chair in the waiting area and tried to read the magazine she had bought hours and hours ago.

When the digital numbers on the airport clock flicked to 4:30, Jamie decided to reverse strategy. She'd call him from here. Ticking the hours off on her fingers, she checked her math. Yes, it was ten-thirty at night in Amsterdam; she'd call the hotel, and even if he was at a late meeting, she could at least leave a message, let him know she was on her way.

Using her phone card, she dialed the number in Amsterdam. A hotel clerk answered.

"Hello? Excuse me, but do you speak English?"

"Yes, of course," the woman answered in lovely, accented English. "May I help you?"

Jamie gave a sigh of relief. She was smiling, holding the receiver with a hand that was wet with excitement. "Yes, please. Would you ring Mr. Rockford's room, please?"

A moment's silence. "I'm sorry, but Mr. Rockford has checked out."

"Edward Rockford?" Jamie repeated, stunned.

"Yes, that is correct."

"But he couldn't have. I mean, he flew home overnight, I know that, but he was returning today. This evening. I . . . I'm sure; he gave me this number," she persisted stubbornly.

"I am sorry, but the remainder of his stay has been canceled."

"Canceled? Did he go somewhere else? To another hotel?" she demanded.

"I am certain he did not. Mr. Rockford always stays with us when he is in Amsterdam. And . . . I am checking my records, and yes, the phone call canceling the room was made from the States."

"Oh," Jamie whispered, dismay making her tongue-tied. "Oh."

The woman on the other end seemed to sense her turmoil. "Hello? Are you still there? Is there anything else I can help you with?"

"No. No, thank you. Good-bye."

She hung up but stood frozen. *Don't panic! Think, Payton . . . it's all up to you now. Think!*

With exaggerated calm she dropped a quarter in the phone slot, called information, and then the network offices.

"Good afternoon. Universal Broadcasting. Can I help you?"

"Edward Rockford's office, please."

"One moment, please."

Okay, she told herself. It's okay. He just changed his plans. "Hello?"

"Hello, this is Donna Frye. May I help you?"

"Yes, Mr. Rockford, please."

"I'm sorry, Mr. Rockford is not in. May I take a message?"

"Are you expecting him?"

"Not this afternoon. May I—"

"Has he been in today? Is he here in America?" She knew she was starting to sound a little crazy, but this was the best she could do, dammit!

"I'm afraid all I can tell you is that Mr. Rockford is not in. But if you would like to leave a message, I will be happy to give it to him when he returns."

"And when will that be?" She pressed her lips together, lowered her voice. "Please, can you at least tell me if he is on his way to Holland or if he is here, right here in town? I have to know whether or not to get on this airplane, and I think they are calling for reboarding!"

"I am sorry, but I—"

"Never mind. Forget it." Jamie clenched her teeth and slammed the phone down, then she picked it right back up and dialed information. Thank heavens he was listed. She dialed his apartment and let the phone ring ten, eleven times . . . twelve. Nothing. No answer. What was she going to do?

Dreading the conflict, she redialed his office. "Ms. Frye? This is important, could you just tell me if Mr. Rockford is here in town? There's no answer at his apartment—"

"I am very sorry," the woman said softly. "But if you would leave a message—"

"All right," Jamie said wearily. "Yes. Fine. If he calls, please tell him that Jamie Payton called and—"

"Ms. Payton? Is this you—Jamie Payton?"

"Yes."

"Oh, Ms. Payton, I wish you had said that when you first called! Mr. Rockford had been trying to reach you for days from Amsterdam. He even had me speak to the phone company. But no . . . he is not in Amsterdam now. He never met the company plane this morning, and then I got a . . . well, an unusual call from him."

"What call? From where?"

"He didn't say. As a matter of fact, he hardly sounded like himself at all. The only thing he would say was that he would not be in. Did not know *when* he would be in. And that he was going away."

"Away? Where? Did he tell you where he was going?"

"No, and I'm afraid I can't imagine—"

Jamie stopped listening. *She* knew where he was, knew it as surely as she knew she loved him, and that he loved her. Panic melted into a trembling joy; he was there, waiting for her, at the house in the woods.

Swiping at her face with the back of one hand, she said, "Donna, do you have the number for his country house? Phone number? Address? Anything?"

"House?" his secretary echoed, sounding completely in the dark. "I'm sorry, but I don't know anything about a country house."

"No, I guess not. Well, thank you anyway. And Donna . . . I'm sorry about hanging up like that before. Really."

"It's quite all right, Ms. Payton. That was nothing compared to Mr. Rockford's . . .

um . . . annoyance when I could not convince AT&T to send a man out to your apartment to replug your phone." The humor in her voice made Jamie smile. She knew already that she was going to like this woman!

"I can imagine." Jamie chuckled.

"Oh . . . I doubt it. But good-bye. And good luck!"

An airline give a refund? She must be kidding.

With a voucher good for a future flight valued at $1,100 tucked in her wallet, along with the little money she had left after wiping out her savings account, Jamie caught a cab for home.

They got as far as the edge of Georgetown before they got stopped by a tangle of rush-hour traffic and construction. A water main had broken; streets were blockaded; cars were stalled. No one was going anywhere.

"Listen, I'll get out here." Jamie sighed, opening her door.

"Oh, thanks a lot, lady! That really helps!"

"Sorry." Adding another single to her tip, she passed the money over the seat and climbed out with her suitcase, leaving the taxi fitted neatly fender to fender in the endless chain of cars.

It was a cool cloudy evening, threatening rain, and Jamie walked along, switching her suitcase from one hand to the other as it grew heavier and heavier, her free hand held out from her body for balance.

She was beyond thinking, beyond planning. The best she could do was get home to the loft. Hope there was a call on the machine, or that he'd call soon. Try his apartment again. And wait.

And if he didn't call? If he had truly given up? If all her saying no had worn him down, driven him away, convinced him that their love was hopeless?

"Never!" She set the suitcase down with a thump. Just stop that, Payton! That's not Edward. It's not! It's you punishing yourself again. Just cut it out! Edward is too strong, too brave for that. No. He is waiting. *You* just have to find him. She grabbed her suitcase again and started walking. The truth is, it's up to you, Jamie Payton. If you love him enough, if you really want to be happy, you are just going to have to find him.

With that thought filling her mind, she turned the corner . . .

. . . and there, halfway down the block,

was the little shop, its sign freshly painted across the window: MYSTERIUM. And propped in the corner of the window, a smaller sign, in square, ordinary little letters: OPEN. PLEASE COME IN.

FIFTEEN

Tiny bells strung on a silver rope jingled as Jamie opened the door.

The little old man looked up from his dusting behind the counter. "Well, well." He smiled, his eyes twinkling. "What a nice surprise."

"You remember me?" Jamie asked softly, setting her suitcase down in the corner.

"Of course I do. You're the artist who bought my paints."

She nodded. "Those were some very unusual paints," she said, carefully watching for his reaction.

He smiled like a cherub. "Perhaps you are a very unusual artist."

She tipped her head, a soft look of discovery washing over her face. "Yes," she said, "perhaps I am."

"And what is it you've been creating, if I might be permitted to ask?"

She opened her mouth to answer, but closed it, thinking. Then with a grin she answered, "A life."

"Ah. A good thing to have." He nodded wisely.

"Most certainly." She nodded back.

And then she did something she hadn't at all intended to do, something that would have seemed quite silly if she had stopped to think about it. She came right out and asked, "Is this a magic shop?"

"Oh," he replied, "I have a few odds and ends of supplies for the magic trade. A top hat complete with rabbit, a—"

"That's not what I mean," she said, stepping closer.

"What do you mean?"

"There's something very strange about this store—"

"Strange?"

"Well," she amended, "mysterious!"

"Ah, from the Latin, *mysterium*—that which excites curiosity and wonder. Of course. But so many things are mysterious. Life is mysterious, don't you think?"

"I certainly do! For example, I came looking for you the other day. I searched everywhere. I swear, we walked up and down every street in this neighborhood, a friend and I, and we couldn't find you."

"I'm so sorry. I try to be here whenever someone needs me."

She blinked, narrowed her eyes to see him all the better. "You do?"

"Of course."

"Then that's why you're here today!"

"If you say so." He smiled again. "Though I hope you aren't here for more paints."

"Why not?"

"I'm completely sold out," he replied, waving his feather duster over the counter like a magic wand. "As a matter of fact, this is quite a coincidence. I thought of you this morning."

Jamie drew in her breath. "Why?"

"A gentleman stopped in. He seemed quite upset. Weary. Despondent. Quite at wit's end. He came in only to ask for change for the telephone, but we spoke for a moment or two, and then he ended up buying the paints."

Everything had stopped. The world was suspended in time and space. Jamie held her breath. "And then?" she whispered.

"And then? Why, he left."

"No! That can't be all," she insisted, hands pressed to the edge of the countertop as if it were the edge of the world. "Did he leave a name? An address? Anything?"

"Well, let me see," the old man said, turning to an old lacquered tin next to the cash register. "He had me mail the paints to a local address, but I do believe he left me a card. Yes, here it is, with an address on the back . . . in case anything else came in which might be of interest to him."

"*Me*," Jamie whispered.

The old man only smiled.

"Oh . . . May I see the card? Please?" She was trembling with eagerness.

And there it was, in her hand:

Edward Rockford,
Vice President, International Division

Quickly she flipped the card over. And there, hastily written in ink, was an address:

250 Hilltop Lane
Mountain Village, Virginia

"Mountain Village?" Jamie read aloud. "Do you know where that is?"

"I believe he said it was in northwestern Virginia. In the Shenandoah Mountains."

"Did he give you directions?"

"No, my dear." The old man chuckled. "He did not expect me to be delivering a gift to his door."

"No, he wouldn't have known. But"—she bit her lip, her eyes shining—"I bet you *do* have a map."

"A map." He snapped his fingers and disappeared behind the counter. She could hear him chanting, "A map . . . a map . . . Let me see. . . ." He popped back into view. "Aha! Here you go—eastern United States. That should help."

"That's perfect!" she exclaimed. "Oh, you are a dear and wonderful man! Thank you—" As she spoke she was already spreading the map out over the countertop, smoothing it with one palm, tracing red and blue lines with the tip of one trembling finger. "Marshall . . . Strasburg . . . Luray . . . Hawksbill . . . Mountain Village!" she exclaimed, dancing with excitement. "Here it is, right here, see!"

"Looks like a lovely spot." He smiled, squinting down at the old, yellowed map.

"Oh, it is, it is! And it will be all golden and crimson now, the trees touched with the first autumn colors, and the sky will be blue and high with white fluffy clouds. And there's a house there, and a man waiting. . . ." She paused and drew a deep breath, her eyes shining with happiness. "He's waiting for me."

And without another word, she turned and picked up her suitcase. "I've got to go rent a car. Good-bye. And thank you."

Which was how, an hour later, Jamie happened to be in the driver's seat of a rented Ford, heading out of Washington and west with the sun toward the Shenandoah Mountains . . . And Edward.

SIXTEEN

The dog greeted her down near the gate where she left the car. She could have raced up the path, *flown* up it on wings of excitement, but she chose to walk slowly, the night air sitting cool on her shoulders like a shawl.

She'd gotten lost twice on small country roads, but people had been so nice. There was always a smile to go with the directions; one woman had even given her a cup of coffee and home-baked cookies.

And now here she was. Here was the house, sheltered among the trees, a single light shining in the front window just a few yards . . . now a few feet away.

Reaching up, she knocked on the door.

There was no answer, just silence. The house sounded empty and deserted. But Jamie was so absolutely sure she was right, it didn't even faze her. She pounded on the door with the side of her fist, a good hard drumming that could not be ignored.

Footsteps. And a familiar voice: "Who's there?"

She grinned. "Dante knows who it is. If you want to find out, you'd better open the door—"

But it was open already, open before she could even finish her sentence. It swung wide and Edward was there, a look of pure amazement on his face, amazement giving way to delight, relief, pain, and wonder, a whole kaleidoscope of emotion washing across his usually composed features. He grabbed hold of the doorframe and held on, his knuckles white.

"Jamie! You're here. How? How is it possible?"

"Aren't you going to invite me in?" she teased, her gray eyes shining. "Aren't you going to take me in your arms and kiss me to death?"

The muscles jumped along his jaw. Breathing hard, he leaned toward her. "Not until you tell me why you're here."

She looked him right in the eye, but all her brashness dropped away, leaving in its place a sweet and fervent candor. "I'm here because I love you, Edward. Because you are my best friend, my lover . . . and the man with whom I want to live my whole life. Because, dear man"—she reached up and touched his cheek—"because I can't live without you any more than you can live without me."

"Oh, Jamie, Jamie darling, do you mean it? Do you? Oh, my sweet, my darling . . . Oh, Jamie." He held her so close she could feel the quick rise and fall of his chest, could hear the harsh rasp of his breath in his throat. "Oh, Jamie, I was afraid you'd let your fears come between us. I was afraid you'd hide from me, from life—"

"I almost did. But see, I'm stronger than you thought. No!" She corrected herself quickly, tipping her chin way up, her eyes shining. "I am stronger and braver than *I* thought I was, than I had been taught to think I was. But you saw it in me. Somehow, no matter how hard I worked at hiding it from both of us, you saw it; you set it free."

"You did it yourself, Jamie," he said.

"Look," she said, cocking her hands on her hips, "don't argue with me. I've had an incredibly exhausting day, a wild day!" She grinned. "I even tried to fly to Amsterdam—"

"You what?" He laughed, smoothing the

hair back from her face with the palms of his hands, holding her head between his hands, bending to kiss her. "*What* did you do?"

"I bought a ticket to Amsterdam, but there was something wrong with the plane and we never took off, and I called the hotel there, but your room was canceled, and I called Donna and she said you never met the company plane—"

"I couldn't. I couldn't bear to put an ocean between us. But I didn't know what else to do."

"Edward, you had done everything. It was up to me." She shook her head wonderingly at her own fears and confusions, gone now like mist, like shadows. "Edward, when I thought you were really gone, I couldn't stand it. It was as if I had held happiness in my hand and thrown it away. And I said no, not anymore! No . . . I want happiness. I want a future filled with love. I want *you*."

"And I want you," he breathed, his eyes shining. He took her in his arms and buried his face in her pale, silken hair, her hair like moonbeams, like stardust. "Oh Jamie, this morning . . . this morning I wandered the empty streets in the city. And I felt such despair." His arms tightened around her at the pain of that memory. "It was agony. I couldn't endure it. I walked and walked. All I wanted to do was go back and talk to you again, convince you . . . shout, scream . . . cry . . . anything, *anything* to make you listen to me. But I was afraid I would chase you further away. I . . . I didn't know what to do. But I had to hear your voice one more time. I was going to call. I went into this store, this little shop . . . and this man . . . he, he seemed to know, to understand without a word. He—"

"He sold you paints. You gave him your card, with this address."

Edward held her at arms' length, staring into her face. "How did you know?"

"I'll tell you later, darling. Now finish the story."

"There isn't much left to tell. I must have gone a little crazy. I don't really remember what I did next, nor the drive up. All I knew was that I had to wait for you here. I knew if you wanted to find me, you'd find me here."

"And I did!" She took his face in her hands and drew it down to hers, kissing his mouth, his eyes, his dark furrowed brow. "I did! Because I can do anything. I can laugh and be happy. I can tell you I love you. I can even read the future."

"Do it," he said, looking deep into her

eyes, his own dark fierce gaze unwavering. "What do you see?"

"I see the two of us together, for all of our lives and beyond . . . every day, every adventure, every one of life's sweet mysteries." A smile began to play behind her eyes. Her voice dropped low, and there were giggles rising there like bubbles in a bottle of champagne. "I see the two of us, just minutes from now, inside this house, perhaps in front of the fire . . . and there is much kissing, much hugging, and some incredible lovemaking. Wait! Don't interrupt. No kissing yet or my crystal ball may fog! Then, when we are too tired to move, too happy to try, I see us lying in each other's arms and planning our future together."

"I hope it includes a wedding. Soon!"

"Oh yes, I see it clearly!"

"And children? Many children?"

"Ah . . . children, definitely. The *number* is a bit hazy—"

He laughed, nuzzling her neck. "Fine. Some things should remain surprises."

"Oh yes. There have to be surprises. And magic. Definitely magic!" She lifted onto tiptoe and kissed him again, a long, lingering kiss that carried them through the doorway and onto the hearth rug.

Breaking the kiss, Edward drew back an inch, his eyes wide with wonder. "You were going to tell me about the little man in that shop, Mysterium."

"Later," she said, laughing as she pressed herself along the length of his gorgeous, passionate body. "It's a wonderful story; I'll tell you later. But," she added with a wink, "I do want to send him a wedding announcement. I think he's expecting it."

THE EDITOR'S CORNER

We are proud to present TREASURED TALES III—four wonderful romances inspired by classic, well-loved stories written by some of the most talented and popular authors writing women's romantic fiction today. Touching, tender, packed with emotion and wonderfully happy endings, next month's LOVESWEPTs are real treasures.

From the supertalented Glenna McReynolds comes **DRAGON'S EDEN**, LOVESWEPT #726, another tale full of passion and intensity. When Jackson Daniels awakens and meets the gaze of a sensual, silver-eyed angel, he can't decide whether the tropical island is his prison—or sanctuary! Fascinated by the powerful warrior who would have tempted a saint, Sugar feels that she was born to be Eve to his Adam. Once Jackson binds her to him with pleasure in a private paradise, Sugar must keep her beloved renegade safe within the haven of her heart. Glenna proves that the most dangerous adventure of all may be falling in love!

The ever-popular Peggy Webb delivers another terrific romance with **CAN'T STOP LOVING YOU,** LOVESWEPT #727. When Helen Sullivan makes her entrance in a red dress that fits like sin, Brick wants to toss his ex-wife over his shoulder and make love to her until she confesses why she'd left him. He's come seeking revenge, but she is still a fire in his blood—and she can't deny her rough-and-tumble bad boy still possesses her heart. Peggy enchants with this delicious story of madness and mayhem, spiced with laughter and steamy with irresistible passion—Shakespeare's *Taming of the Shrew* was never this sizzling.

Patt Bucheister invites you to indulge in some **HOT SOUTHERN NIGHTS,** LOVESWEPT #728. He is brash, brilliant, and too damn sure of himself, but Brett Southern knows the worst: Sam Horn is no gentleman! Determined to use her historic plantation for his documentary, fascinated by Brett's gorgeous eyes, her hands, her lips, Sam finds he wants to do more than just kiss this beauty in a red cape. Once her handsome wolf draws her into his lair, how long will she make him wait until she surrenders? Writing of playful passion and spellbinding secrets, Patt evokes the sultry, sensual heat that kindles the best kind of love story.

For the truly unique, the delightful Victoria Leigh offers **STALKING THE GIANT,** LOVESWEPT #729. Alex Hastings is more than Mr. Tall, Dark and Interesting, Jacqueline Sommers decides—he is all her secret dreams of England rolled into one gorgeous hunk! Romancing her with flowers, tempting her with wicked kisses that taste of forever, he makes her promise to be his—but Jack will climb the highest height, even a beanstalk, to get her sexy giant to admit what he feels for her is love. If true romance is the ultimate fairy tale, then Victoria celebrates its mystery and magic in this delectable story of pursuit and pleasure!

Happy reading!

With warmest wishes,

Beth de Guzman

Senior Editor

P.S. Don't miss the women's novels coming your way in February: **VALENTINE,** by bestselling author Jane Feather, is the newest historical romance brimming with passion and intrigue in the blockbuster tradition of Amanda Quick; **PRINCE OF DREAMS,** from the highly acclaimed Susan Krinard, is a spellbinding romance in which a beautiful woman risks the ultimate temptation . . . love with the sensual vampire who's invaded her dreams; **FIRST LOVES,** by Jean Stone, is a wonderful women's novel about three thirty-something women who rediscover their first loves—with devastating consequences. We'll be giving you a sneak peek at these terrific books in next month's LOVESWEPTs. And immediately following this page, look for a preview of the exciting romances from Bantam that are *available now!*

"An author with star quality . . .
spectacularly talented."
—*Romantic Times*

LORD OF ENCHANTMENT

by

Suzanne Robinson

With every fiber of her being, Penelope Fairfax knew that she should run . . . but she couldn't abandon the achingly handsome stranger who'd washed up on her jagged shore. No doubt he was like the other men she'd come to Penance Isle to escape—the rash warriors whose reckless swordplay left her trembling with fear. Yet when this virile castaway awoke with no memory of who he was, she couldn't turn him away, no matter the havoc he would wreak on her peace—or to her heart. . . .

"Where have you been?" he snapped. "Jesu, woman, my stomach is shriveled with hunger."

Pen's hesitant demeanor vanished in a flare of answering temper. She marched up the steps and stood in front of him, arms folded across her chest.

"If you're strong enough to bellow like an ox in rut, sirrah, you're strong enough to descend to the hall and eat with the rest of us."

Tristan narrowed his eyes and took in the rise and fall of her breasts. He hadn't felt so stirred in—he had no idea how long. Letting his sheet fall a little lower on his hips, he stepped close to her, so close he could feel her heat, and said in a growl, "By the cross, lady, if you'll have me in this sheet, I'll oblige you."

Pen's gaze flew from his eyes to his chest, and then down to the warm, smooth skin of his hip. She made a little sound, then stumbled backward, her color rising. Her step took her to the brink of the stairs, where she tottered and cried out. Her fragile features contorted with terror. Tristan swore and grabbed for her with both hands. The sheet fell as he grasped her by the arms, swept her against the wall and pressed against her as if to prevent her from plummeting down the black steepness with the force of his weight.

They remained pressed against each other, he panting with relief, she shivering with leftover fear. Then she gave a squawk and shoved at his chest.

"Don't touch me!"

She writhed against him, and he felt himself stir. Heedless of the blows with which she was now buffeting him, he set his jaw and tried not to succumb to this sudden arousal. He heard her curse him. Her body twisted. Her hip ground into his unruly part, causing it to leap and buck. He gasped. If he didn't stop her, he would lose all chivalry and lift her skirts right here on the landing. He felt himself twitch again. Catching hold of her upper arms, he lifted her abruptly and gave her a gentle shake that bumped her head against the wall.

"Be still, damn you."

She gaped at him, quivering. Slowly he lowered her to her feet. Their bodies slid over each other, and he gritted his teeth as the slight curve of her breasts caressed his bare shoulder and chest. Her legs slithered down his own, and his rigid sex danced into her skirt, seeking her warmth. Wordlessly she continued to stare at him in consternation.

He couldn't help it. As she settled on her feet, he pressed against her and lowered his head. Using his own special name for her, he whispered hoarsely, "You should take better care, Gratiana." He moved his hips against her and elicited a quick indrawing of breath from her. "Look what happens when you neglect me."

She squirmed and turned her head aside, but he found her mouth anyway. She tried to keep her mouth closed. He smiled against her lips and snaked his hand up to cup her breast. When her mouth opened for a gasp, his tongue invaded. She stiffened, then caught her breath as he began to suck on her.

Tristan felt her body soften, felt her lips

open to him. He was brushing his hips back and forth against her when she tore her lips from his.

"No, please."

He heard fear. The music of her voice was drowned by it. Whatever he might be, he was certain he wasn't a man of rapine and forced submission.

"Aye, Gratiana. A moment."

Tristan turned his face away, setting his hot cheek on hers, and gulped in deep breaths. Then he lifted his head to look into her alarmed eyes and gave her a pained smile.

"If you wish to avoid such encounters, I advise you to find me clothing, Mistress Fairfax."

"Oh."

"Aye, chuck. Now, if you will close your eyes, I'll return to my chamber. But if I'm not clothed and fed in the space of an hour, I'll come looking for you as I am, with no sheet."

"No!"

Her outrage made him chuckle. He stepped away from her. Pen's glance darted down, as he'd known it would. She turned the color of a rose, gave a small whimper, and squeezed her eyes shut. Taking pity on her, he turned, picked up his sheet, and vanished into his chamber. She must have opened her eyes quickly, for she banged the door shut after him.

He heard the tap of her slippers on the stone stairs as she fled. Glancing down at himself, Tristan sighed. He went to a washbowl resting on a sideboard and splashed icy water on his face and chest. He spent the next few minutes calming his rampant urges. By the time Mistress Fairfax knocked on his door, he was resting in bed again with the covers drawn up to his chest.

"Enter, Gratiana, if you dare."

SURRENDER TO A STRANGER

by

Karyn Monk

She trusted him with her life—but could she trust him with her heart?

Sentenced to death, Jacqueline never expected a daring rescue from her filthy cell by an unlikely visitor whose disguise hid a devastatingly handsome British agent. Now the two were on the run —and for as long as he was there to protect her, she felt strangely safe. . . .

Jacqueline seated herself in the chair. It was hard and extremely uncomfortable. She twisted and turned in it a few times to see if she could find a more restful position. She could not. She repositioned herself again, leaned back, folded her arms across her chest and gritted her teeth, determined that, comfortable or not, she was going to sleep. Within a few minutes her whole body began to quiver. Now that she had stopped moving, she realized the room was unbearably cold. She would have to stumble around in the dark again to find her jacket, which was coarse and filthy and smelled offensive.

Loud snoring was rising from the mound on the bed. It was quite evident that Citizen Julien, or whoever he was, had not encountered the least bit of difficulty in falling asleep. Despite the fact that his shoulders were bare, he was evidently quite comfortable. Of course, he did have the advantage of a sheet and blanket.

Noiselessly slipping out of her wooden sabots, she crept through the darkness over to the bed. Citizen Julien did not stir but continued his deep, even snoring. Jacqueline let out a small breath of relief.

The problem was that his hand actually gripped the blanket, making it impossible for her to move it without his knowledge. She would have to get him to loosen his hold before she could proceed. She took a step closer to him and bent down low. With one hand firmly grasping the blanket and her lips positioned just inches away from his ear, she shaped her mouth into a tiny circle and very gently began to blow, a soft, fluttering little breath that made the length of hair lying against his ear begin to dance and tickle him. At first he merely frowned, his eyebrows knitting together in profound irritation. She blew a little harder, and to her delight his hand released the blanket and moved up to scratch the offending ear. Quick as a whip she yanked down the blanket and clutched it to her chest. His tickling problem solved, the stranger sighed and contentedly laid his arm on his chest. Barely able to contain her smugness, Jacqueline turned from the bed to wrap herself in her prize.

Strong hands clamped around her waist with an iron grip, and before she knew what she was about she was sailing through the air and landed with a thud on the mattress beside him. He held her down with one hand and looked at her with amusement.

"There are two lessons you have learned tonight," he remarked. "The first, never assume your opponent is sleeping, unless you have drugged him or knocked him over the head. The second, if it is at all possible, make sure you get a decent night's sleep." Still holding her down, he disentangled her from the blanket and arranged it over both of them. Then he lowered himself to the mattress and casually flung his arm over her, effectively pinning her to the bed. "Now be a good mademoiselle and show me how well you have learned the second lesson," he finished, in much the same tone one would use on a naughty child.

"Let me go!" Jacqueline ordered as she struggled against his hold and tried to sit up.

His response was to tighten his arm around her and haul her even closer against his body.

"It was warmth you were seeking, was it not?" he demanded roughly. "You waste your energy and precious sleep with this nonsense. We still have far to go before you are safe. Lie still and go to sleep." Evidently thinking the matter settled, he closed his eyes.

Mere seconds later a sharp pain assaulted his shoulder, and his eyes flew open to see Jacqueline with her teeth on him.

With a soft oath he pushed her away. "Do you really wish to sleep in the chair that much?" he demanded in a tightly controlled voice.

"It is not that I wish to sleep in the chair, it is that I do not wish to sleep with you!" she hissed.

He was silent for a moment, as if he was somehow confused or surprised by that statement. Suddenly he moved away from her. "Mademoiselle," he began in an incredulous tone, "when exactly was the last time you bathed?"

"How dare you!" Jacqueline spat out as she sat bolt upright on the bed.

"I mean no insult," he swiftly qualified. "It's just that if you are worried about your precious virtue I would like to set your mind at ease. My preference is for women who have bathed at least sometime within the not too distant past. I realize your friend who visited you before me was not quite so discriminating, and perhaps that is what has given you cause for concern." He turned away from her and adjusted his half of the blanket over his shoulder. "You may share this bed with me and rest completely assured that even if you were stark naked and willing, I would not have the slightest desire of laying a hand on you."

A mixture of humiliation and fury boiled up inside Jacqueline. It was true, she realized, she was sorely in need of a bath. But the rooms at La Conciergerie did not include hot water and maid service. How dare this vulgar, low-minded lout comment on the miserable state of her hygiene or tell her boldly that he did not desire her. He was discourteous beyond belief. Still, she had to admit, it did make her feel a little safer. Perhaps in her present condition she truly was offensive enough to repel a man. Well, if so, that suited her perfectly.

"Move over," she ordered sharply as she gave the pillow on what was to be her side a whack.

He sighed impatiently and moved a bit to accommodate her. Jacqueline lay down and primly drew the blanket up to her chin. The space he offered her had already been warmed by the heat of his body. In fact, after a few minutes she found she could feel the heat of him radiating across the scant inches that separated them. It filtered through the coarse wool of her shirt and trousers and warmed her chilled flesh. It had been a long time since she had felt warm in bed.

At home, Henriette used to heat the icy sheets of her enormous bed during the winter with a long-handled brass pan filled with hot coals. That was very nice, but inevitably during the night the effect would wear off and she would find herself huddled beneath a mountain of blankets trying not to move out of the last remaining warm spot. During her long nights at La Conciergerie she had tried unsuccessfully to control the terrible chills that assaulted her every time she crawled into her rickety little trestle bed, fully clothed and with only one thin blanket to offer her any comfort. This unfamiliar sensation of heat was absolutely delicious. It made her very sleepy. She allowed herself a muffled sigh of pleasure and unconsciously huddled closer to its source.

"Good night, mademoiselle."

The unexpected voice jolted her back to wakefulness. With a little gasp she rolled over, moving as far away from him as the limits of the bed would allow.

And don't miss these fabulous romances
from Bantam Books,
on sale in January:

VALENTINE

by the nationally bestselling author

Jane Feather

"An author to treasure."
—*Romantic Times*

PRINCE OF DREAMS

by the highly acclaimed

Susan Krinard

"Susan Krinard has set the standard for today's fantasy romance."
—*Affaire de Coeur*

FIRST LOVES

by the sensational

Jean Stone

What if you could go back and rediscover the magic . . .